Lock Down Publications and Ca$h
Presents

I0564660

SAVAGE
FAMILY EMPIRE
Money
A Black Mafia Origin Story

Written By
PRINCE A. TAUHID

First Edition 2025

Printed in the United States of America

This is a work of fiction. Names, characters, places, and incidents either are products of the author's imagination or are used fictitiously. Any similarity to actual events or locales or persons, living or dead, is entirely coincidental.

Lock Down Publications
P.O. Box 944
Stockbridge, GA 30281
www.lockdownpublications.com

Like our page on Facebook: Lock Down Publications
www.facebook.com/lockdownpublications.ldp

Stay Connected with Us!

Text **LOCKDOWN** to 22828 to stay up-to-date with new releases, sneak peaks, contests and more…

Like our page on Facebook:
Lock Down Publications

Join Lock Down Publications/The New Era Reading Group

Visit our website:
www.lockdownpublications.com

Follow us on Instagram:
Lock Down Publications

Email Us: We want to hear from you!

Preface

The establishing of the Savage family empire began in the year 1954 at the return home of three male cousins from the Korean War. They were Johnny Mack, Cornelius (Hound) and Methuselah (Mickey) in this order in age. The trio were the sons of three brothers. They joined the Army in 1948, serving nearly six years in active duty to the country. Once home again in the seaport city of Savannah, Georgia, the two twenty-four-year-olds (Johnny Mack and Hound) and the twenty-three-year-old (Mickey) were restless and craved action in the underworld ghetto haven of their town. It didn't take long for them to come together on ideas. They then set out with a purpose and an agenda.

They took to running for others and bootlegging moonshine, to operating pleasure houses, fencing and reselling stolen goods, and dealing small batches of cocaine and marijuana. Mickey was the one to first generate a quality clientele base and make beneficial connections with powerful white men, as well as other black men like him, who called shots in the city and made wheels turn how they saw fit. Most notably for Mickey, he forged a friendship and business acquaintance with a white guy who was around the same age as he. This was a promising young prosecutor-attorney who was on the rise. Micky persuaded the guy to trust and believe in him.

The new buddy of Mickey's, a Robert "Bobby" Kavanaugh, was a member of a family that owned a lot of land in the city and county area. They had multiple businesses establishments, held tremendous power, and controlled a fair share of the underworld themselves in moonshine and other illegally produced material. Mickey made runs and conducted pick-ups. The whiskey used to supply the liquor houses and sexual playgrounds operated by the Savage cousins, came from the Kavanaugh clan, by way of Bobby to Mickey. A breakthrough opportunity occurred for the Savage trio. This was the end of part of 1957. They were offered the chance to buy an old warehouse from the Kavanaughs. The place was once a hardware store on the west side of town. Bobby's father previously owned it before relocating the family to the Southern side of the city where more whites populated as opposed to the blacks that the inner areas inhabited.

What the boys had in mind to do with the somewhat small structure was definitely to help put them in a better financial situation and open doors to make legitimate riches and clean up the dirty money that was made elsewhere by them. Mickey convinced Johnny Mack and Hound to envision things in the way he had. Eventually, they all had agreed to convert the place to a worthy juke joint that would also host singers, musicians, big bands, and entertainers—talented black folks who toured the *Chitlin Circuit*—much like the other predominant black cities and towns of the South had to offer, and especially so in Georgia.

In addition, a food shack would be built onto the place to feed the people once they'd gotten alcohol into their system, a sex partner under their arms, and feeling good in the after effect that the experience of partying there at this particular spot would cause.

And so, with this, the Savage boys were on the way to the top of the underworld food chain. They were being led now by Mickey operating as the mind, Hound as the muscle, and Johnny Mack, as the smooth savvy one (the voice of reason) to oversee the two younger cousins. They were now ready to become power players. Or were they? The streets (as it's known) have no love, no mercy, and no glory.

Into The 2000s . . .

Fast forward through the years and into the new millennium, the second and third generation of Savage family hustlers carry on tradition that the fathers and grandfathers had long set in place and envisioned for them. The formation of the Junior Black Mafia occurred with the second line of gangstas, then, in the early part of 2000, the third line made their mark with the *New Black Mafia Incorporated,* thus being more tech savvy and sophisticated in their schemes and their narcotic dealings.

Had it not been for the future thinking of Johnny Mack, Hound, and Mickey, their bloodlines would not have reaped the benefits and street glory that they put in place for them several decades before. The plan was to transfer power to their seeds, that way, they could lead and not have to struggle and go through any other wars and additional chaos as they had. This is to lead to **BLOODLINE OF A SAVAGE . . . SAVAGE EMPOWER. . . SAVAGE FAMILY FOREVER . . . SAVAGE MAMAS . . . etc.** It all begins here.

Prologue

The Chatham County Sheriff's office and the Savannah City Police both received calls related to a body being discovered on the bank of the Savannah River. It was one of a white female, a young model. She'd been raped and murdered by strangulation. The corpse was free of clothing, completely naked.

Norma Elaine Maddox, the name of the victim, was an aspiring eighteen-year-old fashionista from around Savannah. Her dream was to make connections in the business and eventually relocate to New York City to fully pursue a career as a model. She'd generated a buzz there in her hometown of Savannah with agents and glam clothing dealers alike. They wanted to seriously work with her, so that Norma could rip the runway and don the latest seasonal wear.

The final few weeks of summer were still upon them. And recently, Norma posed in swimwear along the beach, prior to her untimely demise at the hands of a diabolical assailant. Her attacker brazenly made the anonymous calls himself—acting supposedly as an eyewitness—and reported to authorities on seeing a blue colored four-door Cadillac Fleetwood with a tail fin rear, down near the bank of the river in the wee hours of the morning. The caller also made mention of seeing two people in the car as it moved along the gravel rock and dirt trail that led to the bank of the water. It was stated that when the car finally left, there was only one person at the time, no longer two, a black male driver, according to the caller reporting.

There were only so many Cadillac Sedans cruising around Savannah at the time, and only a few black male owners of them. So happened, Mickey Savage, was one. He then became a potential suspect in police investigations. A couple of hard-boiled homicide detectives decided to pay the dapper Mickey a special visit. One in their own way.

Wham!

A tremendous death blow was put upon the front door to the home where Mickey and pregnant wife Josephine (aka JoJo) lived. The time was 3:00 A.M. The breaking down of the door by a lieutenant Dickie Flaherty and his partner, Elliot Carson, (a sergeant,) resonated throughout the entire domain. The officers had no official warrant, wore plain clothing, and operated on a *No Knock* basis.

The battering ram procedure was part of a dragnet operation being executed by the police, to potentially lock up any and all for interrogation and placement in a line-up, for *whoever* to come forward to make positive identification at some point afterwards. The particular person (Mickey) was named on more than one occasion.

Detective Flaherty was the first through the door. He had his pump-action shotgun drawn and wave it from right to left then back again, in search of a target.

Pow! Pow! Pow! Pow! Pow!

Mickey fired five rounds from his .38 Special from the bedroom where he took aim towards the direction of the living room door. The lighting was dim, but enough for him to see the intruders invading his privacy. He'd hit Sergeant Carson square in the forehead with a slug, slumping him on impact. Death met him instantly. Lieutenant Flaherty caught three of the slugs to the upper body in the melee. He remained alive, but barely.

Part One

From The Beginning

Chapter 1

June 1958 . . .

The *Chickasaw* Night Lounge was one of those hole-in-the-wall party havens in the South, where you would literally have to be there on the spot to experience the type of euphoric ecstasy and electrifying atmosphere, that the low quality, often thought of as an eyesore by the uppity, truly consisted of. The juke-joint drew crowds of common middle-aged blacks who wanted to have fun and do things over the weekend. And this particular place provided all that to the many who visited and could ask for it.

This place was located on Hopkins Street on the west side of the state's third largest city, almost in the heart of the ghetto, and party goers from near, far and all the between, made it their business to visit at first available opportunity they had. Opening hours were three times weekly— Thursdays, Fridays, and Saturdays—with the place packed wall-to-wall each day, and especially anytime a popular singer would appear, while easing along the Chitlin Circuit performing. Those nights became the most memorable of them all. So much so that envy was brought out from the more luxurious professional and well-to-do white singers and establishments, making for lucrative recording deals by whites to blacks who had a buzz on the circuit, and had personality to cash in on. The Chickasaw had it going on like no other. And the people who checked in to visit were made to feel valued and appreciated for the little money they did have and would spend there, adding to the experience. As with all popular juke-joints, the Chickasaw had a food shack connected to it. When people left the dance floor, they could easily get a bite to eat, of the fried chicken gizzards, French fries, liver, burgers, or a bowl of chitlins and rice. They will be able to mellow out the liquor and beer products they'd gotten drunk on. Overall, it was the music, the atmosphere, the food, and the experience of it all that became most talked about of the place.

The overall vision of the lounge was brought to reality by the Savage trio cousins. Hound eventually headed north to Philadelphia, chasing a female he'd met. An extension of the Savage family had established themselves there as well. Hound was back and forth from the city of Brotherly Love to Savannah since leaving the military. He was more active in the underworld and in the streets than the other two. When the three put their money together to buy the Chickasaw, the rest, as it is said, became history. All of their underworld dealings paid off, and they were able to earn profits quickly. The kind that would go to the benefit of the family.

Johnny Mack Savage prided himself on being a ladies' man of them all, a hustler and also, a power player. He had a nice Buick vehicle to get around in. He became a rolling stone, laying down his hat and manhood with whatever female he decided to be with and make a home. His height was six foot four, and he weighed between two-fifteen and two-twenty. Dark in complexion, he had strong features, was muscular and cut in tone of the muscles

Mickey on the other hand, was a more laid-back personality, quiet, monogamous in nature for the most part, but was known to keep two women in rotation to satisfy his amorous appetite whenever it needed to be fed. Also, he was family-oriented and always prepared for the future. The word visionary fit him very well. Before going into the Army, he and his cousins worked for whites. They sharecropped and physically worked day in and night out to help support the family.

Mickey was six four and a half, weighed two hundred ten pounds, with a dark complexion as well. Mostly everyone in the Savage family had dark hues. He was militant in posture and structure, clean shaven, and maintained a low all-around haircut that he kept mostly under a brim hat. Dude was a suave dresser as well and debonair as ever. He had manners and showed good home upbringings. His desire was to have a family structure of his own some day with a female he would eventually make his wife, no matter where the two should meet.

He had two kids already by a woman he'd met while on a moonshine run to Macon and Albany, Georgia. Her name is Katherine Clark. She birthed Rachel on March 11, 1952, and Elijah, who took his dad's surname on November 2, 1953. Kat took her kids and relocated to Miami, Florida. She had family there. She and Mickey split on good terms and remained friends.

On a particular Saturday night in the summer of 1958, the Chickasaw would host a main attraction of a young hot and outstanding female singer by the name of Sharon "Shugg" Tatum. She'd been tearing up the circuit in Tennessee, Mississippi and Alabama, and now it was time for Georgia, her home state, to hear her out and sing along to her hit song "Do Me No Wrong."

The mere eager audience of black society seeking to be entertained by the sensational Shugg Tatum, was ready to give their money to see her perform on the stage inside the juke-joint, the Chickasaw. Shugg wanted to give them the time of their lives for their hard-earned money.

There were two young females there in the crowd that night. One was fresh from graduating high school one month earlier, and wanted to finally have the opportunity to lay eyes on the singer and witness her perform in person, and if possible, have Shugg autograph a post card she had of the city of Savannah. And maybe speak a few words of wisdom as well. The girls had been informed that Miss Shugg Tatum, was very cordial with all young females and didn't mind talking with them.

Chapter 2

Natalie and Josephine Bridges—siblings indeed—were very excited to have a weekend away from their parents of the hometown city of Eatonton, Georgia, Putnam County. The vacation would be worth their while and also talked about for a lifetime to come, if only they could get up close and personal with Shugg. They both were singing along to the lyrics of Shugg's hit song and relishing in the atmosphere. They loved it.

Shugg pleased everyone. *"You can do me no wrong, only do me right, no missed steps about it, I am surely his type; it pains me like hell, behind the things that you do, but I just can't let go, because I do love you!"*

Her words moved the crowd.

"Sang, Shugg!" shouted Josephine, stabbing in the direction of the stage with her index finger in gesture. "That lady know she can sang, Nat," she said to her sister.

"She shawl can, can't she." The two continued on enjoying what the Chickasaw had to offer them. Little did Josephine know that there was a guy who was attracted to her in a special way. He had his eyes locked in on her from the very moment she appeared, paid her fare at the door, and entered. Not a stalker in the least, just an interested man at the beauty, sex appeal, and "newcomer" impression she put on display.

Josephine had a slim-tight figure, light in complexion due to the biracial blood of her grandmother, was at the height of five foot six, and weighed a hundred and twenty pounds. She possessed pinkish medium-sized lips, a cute, pointed nose, light brown eyes, and natural shoulder-length hair she'd put a hot comb on.

For the occasion, Josephine had on a thin material shin length, lavender-colored dress, black heels, a lavender bow in her hair to match, and a gold necklace with a cross on it, along with a bracelet to match. The jewelry was a graduation gift from her father.

Josephine and Natalie didn't really drink, if ever at all. However, that night, while away from home and their overprotective mean father, the girls felt the need to play grown for a change, loosen up, and finally live a little. They found relief from the pressure their parents had upon them and had plans to party hard the entire three days they were to be in Savannah.

Dressed out in Stacey Adams everything—slacks, shirt, vest, hat, and two-tone shoes—Mickey decided to approach what was the apple in his eye at the time. Long before some other would-be slick talker could make their move and kill his chances.

"My-my-my . . . Sugar pie, honey bunch, sweet and lovely," Mickey complimented the young lady heavily. "And what would your name be, little lady?" he asked, propping a shoulder against the wall next to where Josephine and Natalie stood.

The volume of music and noise wasn't so loud in the particular area of the lounge where they were located. Usually, Josephine wouldn't hesitate to quickly brush away any guy to approach, trying to get familiar with her, but the tall frame and masculine aura of the "daddy cool" handsome dark complexion man who spoke nice to her, was too much to resist. She felt the need to at least let him speak more in his pursuit to work his way into knowing her. Besides, he maturely puffed on a cigarette and sipped from his flask on the very drink Josephine and the sister wanted a taste of—

good liquor. He could now be their go-to person to get them what they wanted. And not only that, but the man who approached indulged in grown man products she'd only seen her father and uncles partake of, like strong cologne, good alcohol, and good smoke.

Mnm-hmm! I like the way his combination smell. Josephine thought of Mickey's cigarette, drink of alcohol, and cologne fragrance.

"My name Josephine. But call me *JoJo* please."

"JoJo you say call you, right? Okay. I can do that."

"Much appreciated. By the way, what's that you drinking on? It smells so good, Mister. Me and my sister Natalie here trying to get us some if possible. Can you help us?"

Chapter 3

Natalie looked at Mickey and nodded her head to cosign what the sister had said.

"Y'all trying to get some of this, huh?" he let out with a slight raise of his drinking vessel in gesture, then offered JoJo a swallow. "Have some?"

JoJo locked eyes with him, cracked a smile, then took the flash and hit it slowly, all while maintaining eye contact with him. She then lowered the chrome container from her mouth, swallowing with a bit of passion to it, and simultaneously passing to Natalie for her to taste the good stuff.

"Good ol' moonshine!" Natalie let out, then hit the drink once more for good measure. She then passed back to JoJo for her to do the same, and from her back to Mickey. He smiled and chuckled at the girls.

"Go 'head. Y'all two finish that up if you like. Plenty more where that came from," he stated with a flare of confidence.

JoJo wasted not a second, she took hold of the flask again then turned it up, saving her sister the other half portion. Natalie gulped it up. Shugg was definitely rocking the crowd to them at that point. The alcohol had the girls feeling good, mellow as could be.

"We love you, Shugg!" shouted JoJo, waving her hands and snaking her neck to the tunes. "You say plenty more where that come from, sir?" JoJo asked.

"Yes ma'am, little lady. Y'all want some more?" he responded.

"Is that a *real* question?" she humored. JoJo then smiled at the same time.

Mickey had no choice but to return a smile of his own.

"I can take a joke. Had to be sure y'all were old enough to drink. By the way, I'm Mickey, one of the people you can thank for having the legendary Shugg Tatum up in the place tonight."

He felt the need to put it out there to really grab the attention of the young one he aimed to impress. The two then politely shook hands.

"Ooh, for real! How so?!" JoJo asked ecstatically.

"Well, if you really wanna know, just be patient 'til the shows over. I can show you better than I can tell you. All I ask for after that, is for the chance to talk to you, and maybe we get to know one another, being that I ain't never seen you around her before," he expressed in a sincere tone of voice, as he got close up on JoJo, towering over her with the tall lean frame he possessed.

"Well then, if all this good ol' jive you talking be the truth, I might be willing to agree to what you're trying to accomplish. Who knows? I might be willing to take it a step further with how good I'm feeling right now off that shine you gave us. And how old are you? And let me hit that cigarette while you at it too!" JoJo said, providing Mickey plenty of eye contact and all the promising feedback he could ever want.

The two smiled admiringly at one another. Mickey passed her the tobacco stick she'd asked to take a toke of. He couldn't stop smiling at the young tender. She made him feel good as a man.

"I'm twenty-seven, young lady. A war veteran. And a man in this world we now live in. What about you? Your age?' he asked.

JoJo and Natalie looked at one another and smiled. Natalie, being the older of the two, knew that the mister attempting to catch her sister and make her his lady, had many years in life over her in seniority, and she was a tad too young below the traditional age limit for a female. Natalie also knew her sister well enough to recognize that JoJo took a liking to the man because of the masculine aura and vibe he displayed. Much like their father—a "man's man."

The look JoJo put upon Natalie was a request of permission to take things to another level with the gentleman, who was well-dressed and seemed authentic. Natalie smiled wildly, granting by way of a nod.

Go ahead. Tell a lie. Make things up. Do what the hell ever. I don't give a damn! So long as he come through on his word about the drink and about us meeting Shugg, Natalie thought.

Mickey needed to now pair Natalie up with someone. Specifically, someone like him so she wouldn't feel left out.

JoJo proceeded. "I'm nineteen," she lied. "And in order for you to get more out of me, I need to get more out of you! More drink that is . . . more smoke . . . and my sister here would like someone to connect with. She twenty-one." JoJo emphatically laid out her requirements for more talk time. "Now shoo! Take care of that please, sir. And don't have us waiting too long," she playfully remarked, taking yet another toke of his cigarette, allowing Natalie another opportunity to do the same.

Mickey laughed like crazy at her antics and eagerness for what he had more of.

Before letting him go, JoJo then gently placed the tobacco stick to Mickey's mouth, between his lips. She had always wanted to do such a thing, after having seen it done many times by those white females to white male detectives in the noir crime films she loved to watch. Mickey smiled from ear-to-ear behind JoJo's gesture and the tender kiss she planted on his cheekbone.

Well, I be damned! That moonshine must have magical touch to it! he thought. *Had to have!*

Mickey then eased away in the direction towards the back of the club to the office where his cousin Johnny Mack and the liquor was located. Shugg still had control over the microphone and the atmosphere. Everyone was having a good 'ol time. The Chickasaw was off the chain! Mickey approached Johnny Mack and related the good news he had.

"Johnny Mack, boy . . . I got two young women out there who looking to drank, smoke, and meet two guys!" he expressed in an excited fashion.

"Boy, you don't say? Why you just now saying something to me?" "I had to find out what they were into first. I did. Two sisters actually. One say she nineteen—the one I want—and the *uttin, quenny*-one, she be the one for you. They ain't from 'round here neither. Two country gals, it seem. Fresh as fish that ain't out the Savannah River!" Mickey made him aware.

"Well, gone on and hook up more drink for 'em, and let's go keep 'em company. See where we can go from that point," Johnny Mack encouraged.

Mickey refilled his flask and also, a second bottle for JoJo. Johnny Mack did the same for he and the female there for him. The two Savage cousins then went towards the Bridges sisters.

Mickey introduced Johnny Mack to Natalie. The two began to talk while he and JoJo did the same, picking up where they'd left off. The conversation between both paired couples intensified with Johnny Mack doing a lot of boasting and bragging. Mickey didn't feel the need to do so. Johnny Mack was only making his character known to Natalie. That's who he was. He had to be gaudy, talk shit, and jive all day. For some reason, Natalie ate it all up—hook, line and sinker.

The real moment of truth was now upon Mickey and Johnny Mack, to show and prove their word of mouth was for real. It was time for them to meet with Shugg and the other singer who performed before her that night, a male. They had to be paid the remaining fee for appearing. The first portion was the deposit to get them there with the promise of payment upon completion of the show.

"Okay. Show's over. And it's time for us to take care of Shugg and our other entertainer. You ready?" Mickey asked JoJo.

"Just the sho' as there's a God in Heaven, I am!" she responded with excitement.

Mickey took a look at Johnny Mack, winking an eye. Johnny Mack smiled and returned a wink himself. The two guys then began to lead the way towards the "business room," the office they'd not long left out of. By the time the four reached the location, Shugg had already made it there with her two security men who were on hand with her at the Chickasaw—Big Bear and Big George—her brother and her first cousin. Immediately upon entering and being that up close and personal with the beloved singer, the two sisters were near star-struck and had to maintain their composure so as to not embarrass themselves, or the two men they now had to impress.

Chapter 4

The dynamics of the occasion now began to change, as Mickey and Johnny Mack had done their part in proving they were for real and not a fraud, nowhere in the least. Mickey, the more articulate of the two between he and Johnny Mack, began speaking to Shugg, while walking up closely and holding JoJo by the hand now.

"Shugg! Gal . . . you *showl* did rock the house tonight, you hear me! The Chickasaw was glad you had no problem coming to please us for a second time," he said.

"Well, Mickey, the *Chickasaw,* is actually one of my favorite places to visit. I felt something special about it the very first time I came here. It's always a pleasure, anytime I get contacted by you two . . . You and ol' Johnny Mack. By the way, where Hound handsome black ass at? Damn, I love looking at him. Mm-mm!" Shugg spoke in her signature sultry tone of voice.

"Hound went up *nawf* to Philadelphia for a little while, Shugg. But I bet if he knew you had the hots for him, he'd hurry and get his ass back down here to Georgia with the quickness," Mickey offered.

"Well, next time you talk to him, you tell him I said hello, and I wouldn't mind seeing him again someday soon."

"Will do."

"And who these two lucky beautiful young ladies you two boys got with y'all here?" Shugg asked of JoJo and Natalie. Johnny Mack felt the need to speak now.

"These two lovely girls here are sisters. Shugg," he let out then put an arm around Natalie's waist. "This one with me name Natalie. And her right there with Mickey named JoJo."

"And they couldn't wait to have this opportunity to meet you," Mickey chimed in. They came all the way from—"

"Eatonton, Georgia, Miss Shugg," JoJo cut in to say. "Me and my sister Natalie give glory to God for this chance to meet you. We love you, Miss Shugg Tatum. We really do."

"Yes, we do, Miss Shugg," Natalie now said as she and JoJo looked on in admiration and cheesy smiles.

"Well, I thank you two, y'all hear? And I appreciate the love from you ladies," Shugg responded with sincerity, then reached into a carry-all tote bag she had with her and withdrew two Savannah city postcards to personally autograph for the two Bridges sisters.

Shugg signed:

The Fabulous Sharon "Shugg" Tatum. The Chickasaw Lounge. Savannah. June 1958

"Here you go, ladies," she said, then handed one to each. "I'm sure y'all gonna remember this night here of June 1958."

"Thank you, Miss Shugg! We sho' will!" the girls exclaimed at the same time.

They hugged one another, jumped into the air, and expressed themselves in excited fashion.

"Okay, now you two, Mickey and Johnny Mack. The rest of my payment, nuccaz! Because I need my bread. And have one of your people get me a bowl of fried gizzards and a side of fries. My ass hungry! All that damn *sanging*! I need a drink too!" she expressed, causing the girls to giggle in laughter.

Shugg kicked off her shoes, sat back in the chair in front of the fan, and made herself at home while Mickey and

Johnny Mack began to count out cash and prepared to pay Shugg. Her small fit frame and caramel-complexioned skin was situated very well in the recliner chair she sat in. It matched her hue in a way.

JoJo and Natalie continued to look at the sensational Shugg in a mesmerized daze. They absolutely couldn't believe what was going on. It was real. They'd met and were now lounging with the vocal goddess whom they idolized in a sense, as a strong powerful black woman, who was making progress in the world and capitalizing off her talent.

"If you two ladies like, you can hang out with me here until I get ready to head back to my hotel room," Shugg said, then took a swig of the small bottle of moonshine Mickey gave her. "Johnny Mack, you and Mickey get them gals something to eat too. I'm sure they may be hungry like I am," Shugg urged.

"We don't mind sitting and talking, and enjoying a bite to eat with you, Miss Shugg," Natalie said.

Shugg, Natalie, and JoJo, all began to converse on female topics, while the guys were busy attending to the needs of the girls and getting the place somewhat situated following a packed night. The occasion had to be one of the most memorable—if not the most—of all moments of their young lives. It would be remembered forever more.

***

The time was late and leading into the wee hours of the night. Shugg had not long left to go to her hotel suite, and Natalie and JoJo were now in the process of doing the same. They had a low budget motel room at walking distance from the Chickasaw. However, the two Savage cousins—Mickey and Johnny Mack—were determined not to let these two get out of their eyesight and return home to Putnam County, without them having a sample of the sweet cherry pie between the two sisters' legs. They had to have them—they felt—either that night once leaving the lounge, or at some point soon. The boys had been simply too nice to them to be denied intimacy. "So, where you two staying while here in Savannah?" Johnny Mack asked.

"We staying over at the Chatham Lodge Motel, not too far away from here," Natalie spoke on behalf of her and JoJo as the elder. Also, because Johnny Mack had an interest in her.

"Walking distance basically," Natalie added.

"Now why would we let y'all walk some place at this time of night?" Johnny Mack responded. "And I got a nice ol' Buick out front there, and my cousin Mickey got a Cadillac. Ain't no way we'll let y'all do that. Won't make no sense, will it?"

"Well, you two can drop us off. But we don't wanna separate and ride in two different cars. We gotta keep together at all costs," said Natalie.

"That's right," JoJo chimed in.

"Okay. Not a problem," Mickey input. "We all can ride in my car. That 'hog' out there big enough to hold all us four, I'm sure. And Johnny Mack's Buick is too. But we taking the hog tonight. And if you two up to it, we all can go to the beach tomorrow, so y'all vacation would be a fun in the sun getaway."

"That sounds like something me and my sister came here to Savannah to do anyway. See the lovely Shugg Tatum like we did, and enjoy our time here. And if possible, meet good men like you two while we at it," JoJo responded on cue.

Chapter 5

The four of them got into Mickey's Cadillac. It was a gleaming blue Sedan Deville, only a year and a half off the lot. He'd brought it from the nephew of his business partner, Bobby Kavanaugh. JoJo had the privilege to ride up front with her now date, while Natalie and her admirer sat closely in the back. Johnny Mack was provided all the opportunity he needed to talk the *"good shit"* he so pleased from that point. He and Mickey had shown and proven what they were all about and now it was the sisters' turn to do the same.

"This a mighty fine car you got here, Mickey," JoJo admired.

"Well, thank you. Maybe one day you'll have the chance to drive it, if you and I work this thing out," he replied.

"Mm-hmm! We shall see," she uttered with a smile.

Mickey smiled along with her at the same time.

Johnny Mack and Natalie delved deeply into conversation. He became relentless in pursuit of what he was after with her, and she sensed it. Her sexual appetite rose behind the charming words being whispered in her ear. The eighteen-year-old loved it. The lie the girls told about their ages in the onset began to catch up with them at this point. Especially so for Natalie. The guys were too advanced in the area than they were. Johnny Mack was ready to do grown folks things that *twenty-one*-year-olds do, the age Natalie claimed she

26

was. The couples were halfway to the motel when the near unthinkable occurred.

WHEEERRRR! The blaring sound of the siren from a police cruiser captured everyone's attention in the car. The blue light atop the automobile twirled slowly as the driver of the vehicle pulled closer to the bumper of Mickey's car forcing him to come to a stop at a faster pace of speed than he normally would. The officer executing the stop was a face of authority Mickey and Johnny Mack were already familiar with, the partner of the cop as well. It was none other than Lieutenant Jimmy Wilkens, aka "Pecan Slim," was what they called him, and veteran cop Roy Tolbert.

Prior to the day, the two policemen had busted a whorehouse and a speakeasy the two boys operated. There was no surprise to Mickey and Johnny Mack that the dickhead cops had a hard-on for them and aimed to get them at any chance they had. Wilkens and Tolbert couldn't quite seem to catch them red-handed for shit in the world.

"License and registration there!" Lieutenant Wilkens barked.

He first beamed the flashlight into the vehicle to observe four occupants, all black. His partner Tolbert, stood at a distance behind him and had his service revolver drawn and trained at the window of the Cadillac, ready to fire away if his superior gave the word.

Mickey noticed who it was. "How you doing tonight, Lieutenant?" he said.

"I said . . . license and registration to this vehicle here, boy! I ain't ask for nothing else! Especially not a greeting from you!" Wilkins growled.

"Not a problem, sir. Not a problem at all," said Mickey.

He then reached to get his credentials. The two girls were now terrified out of their damn minds. They'd never been inside a vehicle and experienced being pulled over by the police, let alone, in a fine American luxury vehicle, while at a distance from home, in a car with two guys they'd not long ago met in a juke joint, and had no idea of who they truly were or was all about. Natalie and JoJo didn't know diddly-squat about the two beaus, and they could potentially be at risk for arrest, amongst other things. Natalie held tightly to Johnny Mack's arm.

"I'm so scared, Johnny. This car legal, ain't it? Not stolen, is it?" she asked in a low shaky tone.

"Everything good, baby. Be cool," he replied to keep her calm.

The lieutenant now had Mickey's identity and paperwork in his hands.

"Step out of the vehicle there, Methuselah!" he ordered.

Methuselah! JoJo thought. *I thought his name was Mickey. So, he lied to me already, I see.*

"Lieutenant, is this really neces—"

"I said, exit the vehicle there, boy!!! And I'm the one talking here. Not you!!!" Wilkens demanded of Mickey, drawing his pistol now.

He slowly got out the Cadillac, hands clearly where they could be seen, as the headlights from the police cruiser were bright as could be.

"Alright. No problem, Lieutenant. Just please, don't shoot. You may or may not know already, I've got two kids I'd love to see grow up," Mickey uttered.

What! He's got two kids he'd love to see grow up! JoJo retorted in her own mind the words to come from the mouth of Mickey himself. *The Good Book says, through ye words ye shall be justified. And through ye words, ye shall be condemned! Now I ain't no judgmental person. I have no right to be. But I must now hold some kind of condemnation towards . . . "Methuselah". . . for the good ol' lie he put on an ol' country gal like me!* JoJo thought further.

"Well, if you wanna see 'em grow up, you best do what the hell I tell you to, boy! Now keep your hands up and turn your black ass 'round!" Wilkens ordered again.

He then grabbed Mickey by his wrists one by one and slapped cuffs on them in the process. The lieutenant escorted him to the side of the street in front of his car.

"Johnny Mack Savage, get your ass out of that vehicle and up against this here car too, boy!" Wilkens now ordered the cousin. "A potential stolen car here, I think," the lieutenant expressed.

He then secured Johnny Mack's wrists and had both Savage boys seated on the pavement next to one another.

"Okay, now to you gals. Get y'all asses out this car and take a seat next to those two. And no talking! You might make me nervous. Who you two anyways? Two newcomers to the whore ring these no good jokers running in this here town? Y'all better not let me find out," Wilkens said.

"Y'all two just keep quiet and let him do his job by running a check. Everything all right," Mickey said to them.

"Yeah, y'all be cool," Johnny Mack chimed in, adding his part.

Everyone remained calm and non-problematic for the two cops who'd stopped them.

Chapter 6

Apparently, the lieutenant must've had the wrong impression of the car that four black occupants rode in, being that he hadn't received a call back from dispatch over the radio as to whether or not the vehicle was valid to Mickey or stolen. He wanted a response in a timely fashion regarding the car's status. Due to the slowness of the report, Wilkens had automatically assumed something wasn't right.

"I figured that if we sat long enough aside the road leading from that damn *'Jungle Joint'* that way," the lieutenant pointed in the direction of where the Chickasaw was located, "that I'd have the opportunity to snag a few monkeys who were up to no good. And then, along came the four of you in a goddamn new Cadillac! Now I know damn well, *nary* one of you bastards holds a job to pay for this here car. It *must* be a hot one!" Lieutenant Wilkens spat.

"No suh, 'Pecan Slim'!" Mickey said. "I actually bought this here car from a nephew of a good ol' friend of mine. Someone I'm sure you may know."

"Now just keep quiet there! My radio will do all the talking I need to hear there, boy! Now *shush* it! Speak when spoken to! And that's Lieutenant Wilkens to you. My nickname is not to be spoken of. And what place you two from? Where's your hometown?"

His aggressive speech was now directed at Natalie and JoJo.

"Who's the oldest?" he further asked.

"I am, suh," Natalie replied. "And we came here from Eatonton, Georgia, on Friday afternoon, to see Shugg Tatum perform. We enjoyed it."

"Um-hmm! You might ah picked the wrong pair of guys and the wrong time to enjoy things. And who is she to you?" he pointed at JoJo.

"She's my sister, suh," Natalie responded, now a little more proper in speech.

"She look kinda underage there. How old are the both of you?" the lieutenant asked.

Reluctant to begin with but had no choice other than to tell the truth to the policeman, Natalie was too fearful to lie to a cop, and dared not think of doing such a thing. The consequences would be too severe if the lie was revealed.

"I'm Natalie. And eighteen. And she's Josephine. Sixteen," she said.

Technically, JoJo was to turn seventeen that year, on Christmas Day. She'd begun school early and graduated ahead of time. Natalie turned eighteen earlier in the year. The lieutenant was provided the majority of their truth.

"And you mean to tell me you two young gals chose these two crooks here . . . these two scoundrels here . . . to show y'all a good time?!" Wilkens mocked and shook his head from side-to-side in disgust.

He had a smirk about his face as well. Natalie felt she needed to think up a quick reasonable response to what the policeman had said to keep him from digging deeper with his questions.

"So far so good! We don't have any complaints about them."

Johnny Mack and Mickey were made to smile in the right way behind her words.

"So far so good, huh," Wilkens said. "Well, if you like it, I love it. Now back to you and you . . . the *Savage* boys!" he pointed from one to the other.

He seemed to despise Mickey more than Johnny Mack, for whatever his reasons were. Mickey was a shade or two darker in complexion. Maybe that was the cause for the disdain in Wilkens.

"Any weapons, drugs, or contraband in this here car?' the lieutenant asked.

"No sir. Have a look for yourself," Mickey said. "It's my car."

"I think I'll do just that," Wilkens responded. "Roy, keep an eye on 'em. All three eyes, okay? The two in your head and the one from your pistol barrel you holding. I'mma search the car. And if I so much as find anything!" he got louder again. "Any dope, booze, or anything—too much tobacco—anything, I'mma lock the both of you black ass jungle bunnies in a goddamn jailcell and let them gals go! You hear me, what I say!" he emphatically stated to Mickey and Johnny Mack.

"Check if you must. Do as you may. But I promise, I can make this situation a whole lot easier, if you willing to contact a significant somebody I'm friends with," said Mickey, offering a compromise.

"Contact a significant somebody? Who?" Wilkens asked, roving from one end of the front seat to the other.

"A man I'm sure you know. 'Bobby Kavanaugh,' the Chief Assistant District Attorney here in Chatham County," Mickey stated, causing the lieutenant to pause his search, and Johnny Mack looking over at him in a confused way.

Truth is, Mickey kept a tight lid on the connections he had, and the people he dealt with. Opposite of black business people, Johnny Mack knew his cousin had serious ties with prominent white clientele, who held top positions in professional circles and well to do society. It was these men of cultivation, Mickey maintained the knowledge of to himself, for situations like the one he now found himself in. Bobby Kavanaugh was such a person.

Chapter 7

Mickey made an arrangement a time ago with Bobby for one of his highest earning working girls. Her name, Evelyn Ayton, affectionately referred to as "Miss Peaches." At any time Mickey had business with Bobby—on a moonshine run dropping off or picking up—Bobby would be holed up at some undisclosed location with his favorite black female he loved to be intimate with. Miss Peaches was kept around strictly for Bobby. Business was always good when Bobby was pleased. He loved the natural stench of Miss Peaches' black ass. He couldn't get enough of it.

Lieutenant Wilkens responded to Mickey's words. "You say, Bobby Kavanaugh?"

"Yes, sir. I did. He witnessed the sale of this car to me. If you don't mind, have main control at the station contact him, then he'll contact you. Mention my name and what's going on. Mickey Savage. That's all you have to do to verify my car not stolen," he stated with a heightened level of confidence.

"You better not waste my time or bullshit me, boy! Mentioning a good man's name like Bobby's. Not in the least, you better not," retorted Wilkens.

"I promise you, Pecan Slim, I won't. And by the way, how'd you get that nickname?" Mickey had the audacity to ask.

"That ain't none of your goddamn business, boy! *That's* how I got it! How 'bout that!"

The commanding officer then stepped out of earshot from everyone and called over the radio to dispatch. There wouldn't be a problem being able to contact the ADA. The station had the direct ability to do so. After a five-minute interval taken by Lieutenant Jimmy Wilkens, he returned to the presence of the four seated along the curb. He then began to speak on his short-lived investigation, while taking the cuffs off Mickey and Johnny Mack.

"I want to apologize to you nice people here tonight. There's been a great misunderstanding here. Everything checked out properly. You may be on y'all way now. And you two girls please continue to enjoy all the goodness that this city has to offer, okay? Take care folks!" Lieutenant Wilkens said, as he looked Mickey and Johnny Mack directly in the eyes, prior to he and his partner, Roy, getting into the police cruiser and leaving fast.

Johnny Mack, Natalie, and JoJo all looked on at Mickey with an expression of shock and surprise. Their eyes were bucked and mouths wide. No one could believe what had just happened. Mickey was the second coming of Christ in that moment.

"Mickey Elijah Savage! What the fuck type of rabbit you just pulled out your ass there, cousin?" Johnny Mack said. "Now who the hell you know? Talk, nigga!"

"Never mind, cousin. Just neither one of y'all," he went back and forth with a finger in gesture from one person to the next, "better not ever repeat the name y'all heard me say to the policeman. Not ever! Okay, Johnny Mack? And I mean it from hell and back!" Mickey demanded obeisance from them all. "Are we understood on that?"

The others complied in unison. They then got back into the Cadillac and continued on about their way, with JoJo holding a continued mesmerizing look about her face with a smile, and not for once taking her eyes away from Mickey.

JoJo knew then and there that the one particular Savage who wanted her, was going to high places in realms of power and calling shots of his own. She began to draw closer to him, beginning that night. Also, the beginning of her trust in him to always do the right thing. It didn't take much. And that was all she needed to see to know he was really *that* dude. Her attraction to him had grown tremendously.

Chapter 8

Finally, the four arrived at the motel. Mickey steered the big, beautiful luxury sedan into the parking lot like he was the president, driving the car himself and in no need of a chauffeur, not in the least need of one.

"We here, y'all," Johnny Mack let out. "No mo trouble with the law."

"Amen to that," commented Natalie.

"Ain't that the truth," JoJo chimed in to say. "I was so scared y'all. Outta my mind, scared."

"Me too, JoJo. You know where we from, you ain't gonna ever see many Negros with a new Cadillac. And damn sho' not *four* of them riding in one, getting stopped by the 'man' and riding away like they ain't never get pulled over in the first place. But obviously, ol' Mickey there took care of everything and saved us from trouble. Now it's on us to take care of them," Natalie said.

She was hot between the legs and ready to have sex. Johnny Mack had already eased his hand under her dress and toyed with her goodie box. He knew what it smelled and tasted like already. She was warm and wet to the touch. Now the time was at hand to know what Natalie felt like while his manhood was hung deep inside. He would be the second dude to have her, if all continued to go well. Everyone got out then casually walked to the door of the room the two sisters stayed in. Natalie had the key. She unlocked and opened the door.

"Welcome to our resting place for the weekend, Johnny Mack and Mickey," Natalie said to them with a smile.

The guys looked at one another, then put their focus back on the girls. They both returned smiles of their own. The room had twin beds set inside. Not too big or too small. The boys had no plans to be there long no way, at least not that night, not for a prolonged period of time.

"Which one you sleeping on, Natalie?" Johnny Mack asked.

"The one I'm headed towards now," she responded.

It was the one on the far end near the bathroom. JoJo needed to relieve herself. She's been holding on to that moonshine for quite a while now. Upon entering the room, she headed straight that way. Natalie was next to go herself.

How shall I go about this? I like Mickey. Indeed, I do. And I'm more than sure he's capable of taking care of me, if I give into him. An older man is always qualified. He and Daddy are one and the same. I really do want a boyfriend in my life. Someone I can relate to and grow in life with. A guy around my age though. But having a "grown man" is good too. However, a grown man is always ready to be grown. Do grown man things with young gals like me and make babies. Just like Mama and Daddy and Grandma and Granddaddy. I don't know if I'm ready for babies yet. I do want to enjoy life by myself for a time being without kids. But I know Mickey a good catch, an outstanding one for me. And I can't allow him to pass me by. My ass just scared really and unsure what to do, she thought.

JoJo had a long conversation with herself to try to come up with a solution to the personal dilemma she now faced. Something had to give. Because Mickey wasn't going to be around too long waiting for her to make up her mind. She wiped, flushed, washed her hands, then exited to find Natalie and Johnny Mack half-naked and frolicking about atop the bed. They were taking things to the next level already.

"Nat. You two ain't waste no time, did you. My God! And where Mickey go off to?" JoJo asked.

"He say he want more privacy for you and him. I think he gone to get a room for you two," Natalie responded.

Johnny Mack now had her panties halfway down her legs as she lay back and allowed him to do as he pleased. Her dark-colored wedge sandals were already unbuckled and taken off. Her dress as well. All left to keep her lady ornaments covered was her bra and panties.

"Wanted more privacy, huh?" JoJo uttered in a low tone of voice. *That's what any gentleman would do,* she thought.

"Johnny Mack, hold up a moment please," Natalie said. "I need to use the bathroom." She then hopped up and made her way to relieve herself. JoJo followed.

"What you plan on doing, JoJo? Stay in here and watch me and Johnny Mack? Or head on out there to meet Mickey, and y'all two go on to another room?"

"Well, my gosh," JoJo responded. "I guess I'll head out to meet Mickey. Then we get our own room. Because you two have clearly taken over this one," she further said with a laugh and a smile.

"Thank you!" remarked Natalie, returning a smile of her own.

JoJo then exited. Johnny Mack wasted no time in getting asshole naked as he awaited Natalie to come out. The two of them was about to do the nasty.

JoJo walked towards the window where reservations are made. Mickey's car was still parked in front of the room. She knew he was close by somewhere. Her eyes then laid on him. He was walking back in her direction. He had a look of disgust about his face.

"What's the matter, Mickey?"

"No more rooms available. We're not able to have a private moment. To talk really. You're too innocent for me to try to sleep with. It's too soon. I've got more respect for you than that."

JoJo locked eyes with him as he stood tall, towering over her in height. She rubbed on his left arm gently.

"I understand. And I appreciate the level of respect you got for me. I really do. Whether you know it or not, you're the one I want. You've convinced me. I now feel like I don't need to look no farther. I've found him. And that's you. My heart, gut, and my spirit has never failed me. Not in the least. It's a unanimous decision on this. You win. And I'm the prize," JoJo confirmed.

She then pulled Mickey down to her level by the back of the neck and gave him a passionate kiss. The young girl was inexperienced and didn't know much in the area of romance. She just knew how to imitate what she'd seen in those noir romance films she loved to watch. The two then walked to Mickey's car and took a seat inside. They kissed more. She took hold of his hand and guided it underneath her dress, situating it directly on her warm kitty between her legs. This personal space was a sanctuary. A place no man has had the pleasure to explore.

"Mickey, the inside of your Caddy here is a private enough place for me," JoJo said.

She slipped off a shoulder strap of her dress, then the other, exposing those barely there B-cup breasts of hers. They were firm and sitting properly in place.

"I know somewhere we can go," he said, then fired up the hog, geared it to reverse. Backed out the parking space, geared to drive, then pulled off, headed to a low key location.

Throughout the ride, JoJo sat topless and close up on Mickey. The warm summer night air and the euphoric energy the affair with him provided caused both of them to feel so good.

Shortly thereafter, the familiar smell of port water and marine life permeated throughout the car. Mickey pulled onto a narrow gravel rock pathway. It led to the bank of the

Savannah River. The bright near-full moon illuminated the night sky and reflected atop the water. The slow flowing current and the minute wave ripples banged against the shores leisurely. The sounds were calming. Mickey parked facing the water. The great state of South Carolina could be seen at the distance across.

"How you like this spot here to chill for a moment?" he asked.

"I think it's nice. Really laid back. Really quiet and peaceful. And it's just the two of us. Never been on a date down by the river. Only to do laundry. But it's a first for everything."

Chapter 9

They talked a little more. Mickey felt the need to do so to calm her and to establish a level of trust. He detected a small level of fear. His understanding knew why that was so. Any teenage girl all alone with a grown man, in a dark area of town not their own, would feel the same way. Mickey was no predator by far. Nor was he a threat. He made sure to communicate his feelings to her in how he perceived the way she might have felt. Their conversation got deep. She had a few questions for him. Some he'd anticipated.

"So, how long it's gonna be before you told me you had two kids? *Methuselah*." JoJo had heard the cop call him by name.

"I was gonna say something about it in due time. Had to wait until my interest level in you got higher. But now that you've brought it up, I've got two kids and have never been married. A son and daughter. Me and their mother wasn't able to make it work. She wanted me to be the type of man she wanted me to be. And I wanted to be the type of man I wanted to be. And that's what happened. She moved on to find the man she wanted. Or attempted to. And I moved on to become the man I am, Mickey Savage. A patient man who was provided a sporting chance in the world I play. And a jack of all trades," he spoke clearly and confidently.

"Um-hmm! Mister 'Jack of all trades!' How did I get so lucky?"

"How did *you* get so lucky?" he retorted with a smile. "I should be asking myself that. And I bet you ain't never even been touched before, have you?"

JoJo smiled at his question. "Nope. All virgin. So fresh and so clean. But my ass wanna be touched. Tonight though. O this wee hour of the morning, I shall say."

JoJo then slipped off her panties and was now completely naked. She climbed over the seat and got in the back. Mickey followed her actions. They were both naked in this moment. The grown man version of him began to show. He took total charge of the affair.

Mickey tenderly touched on her breasts and private area. He used both his hands and his lips to stimulate her. He then positioned himself over the creamy chocolate heartthrob and situated the head of his love tool at the opening of her tight box. His cannon was large, leaving him eager to take charge.

"Oh, wait!" JoJo said, causing Mickey to look confused. "My shoes. I've gotta take them off. Don't want to dirty up this nice car you got here," she said with a laugh.

He had to laugh himself. They both began to unfasten the brown wedge sandals she had on to match the dress she wore. Strong passionate glances were made. They smiled as well. Their hand speed was fast, very eager to get to the business. The fragrance of each other's natural body musk invaded their nostrils. Their sexual excitement was to the max.

JoJo then lay back and spread her legs wide. "Now back to this part. Let's do it," she let out in a happy state of being.

Mickey spared her no more. He penetrated and popped her sweet little cherry. He became the first. A moment to be remembered for a lifetime to come.

Chapter 10

Mickey and JoJo returned to the motel room. They found Natalie and Johnny sound asleep. His chrome-colored flask lay flat atop the nightstand. The two had fucked, downed a good amount of moonshine, then fell fast asleep. A pleasing combination any couple would take advantage of. JoJo and her date went to the bathroom to wash up. JoJo needed a warm soapy washcloth between her legs. Dude had put it on her real good. He loved it. So did she. They exited the restroom and took off a few pieces of the clothes they had on. It was time to rest.

***

Everyone had awakened around noon. Mickey and Johnny Mack went home temporarily to bathe and change clothes, leaving the two sisters there to talk amongst themselves while they were away.

"Okay JoJo, you first," Natalie said. "Where did y'all go and did y'all do anything?" She wanted all the juicy details.

"Sisss!" JoJo let out excitedly.

The very thought of Mickey taking his time to stroke passionately and loving her in the right way, sent tingles racing up and down her spine. She was somewhat sore but ready to do it again.

"He took me to a spot down by the river. We made out in the back seat of his car. That also turned out to be a good time to sit, talk and get to know one another. That was the most important part before we got to the other important part. And Nat," she said, then took a pause and raised her eyebrows, producing a look of satisfaction about her face. "He's a *man* too, sis! I mean a MAN! Had my little hot ass damn near about to push myself out the backdoor of that Caddy."

Natalie giggled like crazy at her sister's remark. "So, you finally got that little cherry of yours popped, huh?" Natalie commented, smiling and chomping gum. "Now all you gotta do is keep the 'dick monkey' off your back, because those urges will be hitting like crazy and have you wanting it all the time from here on out. Sex is addictive, JoJo. You gotta control yourself at all times," Natalie cautioned.

"If I can have anyone when I want it, however I want it, Mickey gonna be the one to give it to me. He surely will be."

"And how you plan to make that happen? Because you know you won't be able to while still living in Eatonton under Daddy's roof. You know better than to think like that."

"That's the thing. We grown now, Nat. It may be time for us to move out and live our lives like we want to," JoJo said in a way to try to encourage her sister to think of ways they could pull off such a thing.

"JoJo, what you trying to get me to do? Commit suicide or something?"

"What you already got in mind to do already. Let's stay longer in Savannah so we can spend more time with our new men," JoJo bluntly let out.

"You know me better than I thought," Natalie responded with a smile. "And if that's what you wanna do, then . . . let's do it."

The sisters continued to discuss many things while they lounged around and relaxed in the room. The boys promised to take them to the beach. And the beautiful one Savannah had awaited them. They were ready to have fun in the sun and slide through the city. Why should all the white guys and gals have all the fun!

At the time, blacks could now enjoy the summer sun and have Savannah fun with the ruling of Brown vs Board of Education three years prior. That opened the doors to a lot of wonderful things in this great country, especially so in the South, in Georgia particularly.

***

The Savage boys returned about an hour later. They were in Johnny Mack's Buick now. It was his turn to put on and have Natalie ride in the front seat. The four of them hit the road headed to the beach. A twenty-to-thirty-minute ride from where they were.

"Johnny Mack, this is a really nice car *you* got here," complimented Natalie. "It ride smooth too."

"Thank you, Natalie."

Everyone continued to chat and listen to music from the radio as they rode. They reached their destination, Tybee Island. Upon exiting the car, they hit the boardwalk and stepped into a shop that was lined along the beach. The establishment sold swimwear. Both the girls picked out two-pieces. The color matched the flip-flops they had on. Johnny Mack and Mickey picked out a pair of shorts and flip-flops themselves.

The weather was sunny and nice that day. It was ninety degrees. They all ran from the shop across the sand, and into the water. The girls were having so much fun on their time away from home. They were treated like royalty by the two Savage cousins. Things was going so good for Natalie and JoJo that they really didn't want to return home to their overbearing father and the load of work in and around the house that awaited them.

Truth be told, the two sisters had every intention in the world to go up against their daddy and force him to put them out. One was eighteen already and the other near that. They wanted to get a place to stay together, in Savannah if possible, and have their boyfriends pay their bills until they were situated on their own with a job and whatnot. Luckily for them, they both found a man at the same time. And not only that, the men they now had were related. A win-win situation for the girls.

***

They returned to the motel room right at sunset. Once inside and seated, Natalie broke the news to the boys on what they had plans to do. She first needed the advice of the guys before her and JoJo made up their minds completely on what to do.

"Johnny Mack. Mickey," she called out to get their attention. "Look. Me and JoJo was supposed to get on the bus tomorrow and take our behinds home. But that won't be happening now. We're having too much fun. We met y'all. We've found trust in you two. And y'all treats us right. So, we plan to stay a little longer. Ain't that right, JoJo?" Natalie said.

She needed her sibling to co-sign her remarks.

"Yep! That's what we want to do. Stay here in Savannah with you two. Until further notice."

Mickey took the initiative to speak first.

"You say what? Stay a little longer than you was supposed to? You think y'all daddy gonna be okay with y'all breaking his rules?"

He shook his head in disgust at the idea.

"I don't think that's a good idea, JoJo. But that's just me," Mickey said as he stood to his feet to leave.

"Mickey, where are you going?" JoJo responded.

She seemed to now be in fear behind the plan her and Natalie had in mind. She thought she'd pissed him off.

"I'm going home for a little while. I'll be back later."

JoJo ran over and grabbed Mickey by the arm to hold him up momentarily. She then got a shirt and a pair of pants to put on.

"I'm going with you," she let him know.

"Fine by me, We need to talk anyway about your plan to disrespect your daddy. That ain't good."

"I'll be back, Natalie," JoJo said.

She and Mickey then walked out, got into his Cadillac, and made their way to his place. While in the car, their conversation continued. He wanted to be clear with her on how he felt about their plan.

"JoJo, that's not good, baby girl. To go up against your daddy. I don't like it. Not at all."

JoJo sighed behind Mickey's words.

"I understand, Mickey. I'll go back home tomorrow like I'm supposed to. But what I'm supposed to do when I wanna see you? Spend more time with you? Or when I wanna do it again? It felt good. You done got me started now. So, we got to keep it going," she said.

Chapter 11

There was a meaningful tone to her voice. Mickey took a look at her. A smirk came across his face. Then that smirk turned into a smile.

"How about I got a better idea?" he proposed.

"I don't even have to hear it to know it's a good one. But go ahead."

"Since me and you off to a good start, how bout I take you home. And me and your daddy have a talk while I'm there?"

"Mickey! My daddy'll kill me! Natalie too! Oh no! I can't do that," she detested the thought.

"Well . . . which is better? Me taking you home and having a man-to-man talk with your daddy, and he kill you then? Or, you not going home on time like you 'spose to and he kill you later? Pick your poison. By the way, I'mma remind you, I got a daughter. And I believe I'd respect it better if she brought a guy home and let me meet him and have a conversation, than to disrespect me and not come home on time like I told her to be. That way, your daddy can't say you got outta line," Mickey explained it to her.

"You know what? You're right. You make a good point. Daddy won't be able to say I went against him if I let you take me home. So, I'mma let you and Johnny Mack drive us home. Natalie got some explaining to do too. And just so you'll know, my daddy ain't got to know anything about us having sex either. Okay?" JoJo pleaded with him.

"If he ask, I gotta tell him. And you actually think your daddy crazy enough to believe you ain't slept with a man who brought you home? In a *Cadillac* at that?" Mickey said with a laugh. "You something else, girl. You know that?"

"I can be. At times. But did you hear what I said? Before we started to talk about my daddy?"

Mickey took another glance at her and smiled again.

"Nah. I ain't hear you. What'd you say?"

He wanted to banter in word play. He desired to hear what type of comeback she had.

"I said . . . I wanna do it again. I wanna hunch some more. It felt good to me, Mickey," JoJo expressed.

Her youthful innocence continued to rule over any potential vulgar thoughts.

"You wanna do again, huh? What have I created? A female Frankenstein? I hope not."

"Well, you're the man who took my virginity. You're the reason I'm now sexually activated. You're the man who gave me my first experience. And now, I'm all yours. I want us to have more of one another," she willfully admitted.

Mickey continued to smile. They reached his place and went inside. He had a decent one-bedroom pad to rest well in.

"Make yourself at home. I'mma take a bath and put on a better set of clothes."

JoJo wandered towards the kitchen. Neither one of them had eaten a thing.

I know he's gotta be hungry. Hell, I am! she thought.

She took a look into the food cabinets and the fridge to see what he had she could cook for them. Something quick would do. Mickey loved breakfast food. That was what he had on hand. JoJo took out the particular items to cook, prepped, and then hooked it up. It was grits, cheese eggs, sausage, and toast. There was orange juice to wash it down.

"It smell good in there, girl," Mickey complimented.

"I'll have everything ready by the time you get out the tub, suga. I'm on it, okay?" she made him aware. "I'm here to please you. And to keep that way."

Shortly thereafter, Mickey completed his bath and made his way to the kitchen where JoJo was. They ate the food, sat in front of the TV and talked while they watched the baseball game that was on. JoJo wanted to hear some music. She got up and walked over to the record player. Mickey had a large collection to choose from. She pulled out an album by Billie Holiday. The intense emotional vocals took possession of the atmosphere and mood. She couldn't hold back. The burning desire she developed to have sex. Baby girl was hot between the legs. And it showed. Mickey laughed like crazy at her because he knew what her body language was signaling. He'd popped enough cherries in his time to have his own flavor of soda named in that honor, *Mickey's Cherry Pop!*

He was that type of dude, and it felt good to him to be in the position he stood with females. As for JoJo, he liked her. She would be his special young tender.

"You wanna give me more of that *thang* of yours?" JoJo purred sensuously in his ear.

He turned his head in her direction, locked eyes, and smiled.

"Look, JoJo. I don't intend to continue to give you the best of me, and you're not even my girl yet," he said to her.

"I'm here with you and giving you the pleasure a man want, ain't I? So how am I not yours? As you put it?"

"Because. I ain't met your daddy, for one. We not married yet. And I want more babies. That's how."

He had yet to release himself inside her, only onto her belly, out of fear of getting her pregnant.

"It's marry before you carry, JoJo, and I don't want to put you in no messed up predicament. I don't wanna repeat what I had done wrong with my two kids' mama. I wanna be a married man."

"Well, just do what you did last time and put it on my stomach. Do as you must. Take me as you please. I don't care. Just give it to me. Okay?"

She then began to get naked while standing in front of Mickey. Her short, kinky pubic hairs permeated her natural musk fragrance from the wetness between her legs. The aroma aroused him. He held back no longer. They completed another episode of sex. Mickey let go of yet his second robust load of baby making liquid onto her caramel-complexioned belly.

An hour later, the two returned to the motel where Natalie and Johnny Mack were. They were laid out on the bed asshole naked and sound asleep again. Food wrappers were on the floor next to the bed. JoJo and Mickey didn't bother to disturb them. They simply turned around and walked back out, chuckling along the way. They went back to the beach. JoJo wanted to see the ocean at night and observe the moon illuminated atop the water. She was amazed at how beautiful the surroundings were.

"Now this, Mickey . . . the city of Savannah, and the beach, is something I could get used to and eventually call home," JoJo said in admiration.

She stood barefoot along the edge of the water. The waves washed over her ankles. The ebb and flow dictated by the tide controlled the momentum.

"If everything continues to go as I believe it would, this may very well be your city to live in," he said to her.

"I like the sound of that," she responded, then turned to face him.

They kissed. Their chemistry was there. All that was left for them to do was to get to truly know one another on a personal level and see how far they could go from there.

Chapter 12

One Day Later . . .

The day was upon Natalie and JoJo to return home. Mickey had a conversation with Johnny Mack. He needed him to convince Natalie that it was best to go home and not go against their daddy. JoJo was already in check. Now it was her sibling's turn to get that way. The Savage boys knew it was best to be gentlemen about the whole affair.

The double couples took two separate cars, Mickey and JoJo in his Caddy, and Johnny Mack and Natalie in his Buick. The Bridges' house was located just on the outskirts of Eatonton City Limits in the county area. Upon arrival, the younger siblings of Natalie and JoJo, two girls and two boys, were spotted out front of the house playing. They admired the vehicles pulling up.

"Them two mighty fine cars there, Peanut," said Ted, the elder of the two.

They played one on one football together and paused momentarily.

"They sho is, Ted," Peanut responded. "I wonder who they is? Coming to visit us?"

"Ted and Peanut!" Sasha called out. "Y'all see them two good-looking cars pulling up to our house?"

"Yeah! We do. Who they be?" Ted responded.

"We'll find out in a moment, now won't we?"

Jackie, the twin to Peanut and the youngest of them all, only stood motionlessly and marveled at the luxury mobiles. Natalie honked the horn of the Buick. She then yelled out their names. They recognized her voice and knew their older sibling was back home. JoJo sat in silence in the Caddy, mostly out of fear.

"That's Nat, y'all!" yelled Sasha.

"That's Nat and JoJo!" Ted corrected upon noticing the other sister in the rear car.

"Hey, y'all!" JoJo greeted.

The cars parked and the girls got out. All six siblings then came to huddle and hug one another.

"Hey. Me and JoJo want y'all to meet these two guys here," Natalie said. "His name is Johhny Mack," she pointed "and his name is Mickey."

"Like Mickey Mouse?" asked Peanut out of curiosity.

"Yeah, Peanut. Like Mickey Mouse," JoJo responded now with a smile.

"Hey, Mister Johnny Mack and Mister Mickey!" they all greeted in unison.

Their mother, Martha Jean Bridges, then came to the door. She stepped onto the porch with her hands planted on her hips. She had on a long, loose-fitting floral dress. It looked like a gown. There was a stern look directed at Natalie and JoJo. Her demeanor displayed disappointment.

"Mama, we're home," declared Natalie. "On time too. Just like we supposed to."

Everyone got quiet. They only looked at one another. The young siblings looked from Natalie to their mother, awaiting a comeback.

"Um-hmm! That's not all you two hot heifers have done. Who y'all got there with you, in those cars to help you get home on time? And don't give me no shitty lies. I want it straight!" their mother demanded.

The heads of the four younger siblings then went back to Natalie from their mother.

"Well, Mama. Truth be, this here fella name Johnny Mack. And his name Mickey," replied Natalie.

She gestured from one to the other with her finger. Martha Jean now scornfully looked on at JoJo. She stood close to Mickey and obviously gave it away.

"Apparently, he must be her date?" Mama questioned, nodding with her head at Mickey.

The kids' heads now went back to their mother, then, to Natalie again.

"I can't lie for you and—"

"Answer my question straight, Natalie!" Martha Jean cut her off and demanded.

"Yes, Mama. He is," Natalie responded.

"And this guy your date?" she asked, referring to Johnny Mack.

Natalie dropped her head. She became reluctant to answer but had no choice. The gangsters continued to look on at Natalie. They awaited her reply.

"Yes, Mama. Everything you assume. This is what it is with me and JoJo."

The kids' heads now shot back to Mama. She began tapping her foot on the wooden porch floor.

"The eye test never fails. What you gotta say for yourself, Josephine?"

The young ones looked at JoJo now. JoJo's chin slumped to her bosom. She then spoke with her head hung low.

"Mama, I met somebody I like. Mickey been good to me. He's the one to talk me into coming home on time. Because we wasn't at first," JoJo let out, revealing the original intent.

"You don't say," her mother remarked. "You kids shoo! Get back over there and go play!" she roared.

The four young siblings scurried away with the quickness. Mama meant business.

"How you doing, Ma'am? My pleasure to meet you," Mickey greeted first.

He stepped forward to shake her hand.

"Yes, hello! How are you, Ma'am? Definitely a pleasure to meet you," Johnny Mack followed his cousin's lead.

"I'm well, thank you two for asking. Why don't y'all two come in? That way we'll have the chance to hear each other out. Because I got a hunch that a fresh cherry done been popped. And on the other hand, one done got a different piece of meat for herself." Martha Jean was blunt and blatant with her choice of words.

Natalie and JoJo's father, Teddy Bridges Sr, aka "Boot," wasn't home yet. His workday didn't end until 4:00 P.M. The time was only 2:30. It was the perfect time for the four of them to relate their whole story to Mrs. Martha Jean Bridges.

Two hours later . . .

Their father, Boot, made it home from work. He took notice of the two gleaming luxury automobiles as he pulled up to his house in his overused Ford. The Cadillac and the Buick made his ride look like a joke.

Now who the hell could this be, at my house in those good-looking cars there? Boot thought.

Everyone in the living room took a look out the front door at the sound of Boot's car arriving.

"They goes y'all daddy. You better pray he ain't had a bad day at work. It's Monday too. Lord knows how he may react."

"Martha Jean!" Boot yelled out the moment he got out the car.

55

Chapter 13

His four young children all ran up to greet him and offer hugs. Their actions might have helped to take the sting from how he would react. Although the two boys whispered to him that the company they had was Natalie and JoJo's boyfriends.

"I'm in here, Boot," the wife responded. "We've got company too."

"I see. Who is it?" he asked while walking towards the front door.

He was anxious to know who visited. Johnny Mack and Mickey both stood to their feet upon Boot stepping into the house.

"Good day, sir. How are you?" the well-dressed gentlemen greeted together.

"Who the hell you two?" Boot exclaimed.

He then took a look over at his wife and two daughters. No one answered him. Partly from fear. Partly due to the girls wanting their mother to speak on their behalf. Wasn't going to happen that day.

"I'm Mickey Savage, sir."

"—He's JoJo date," Martha Jean stated. She then pointed towards Johnny Mack. It was an indication for him to speak up now.

"And I'm Johnny Mack, sir."

"—And he's Natalie's date. Thank the Lord for that!" Martha Jean professed, obviously relieved that Natalie could now move out the house and go on about life.

"What!" Boot obliged loudly.

No one said a word farther. The three men continued to stand.

"Run that by me one more time, Martha Jean!" Boot demanded.

"I'mma let them speak for themselves, Boot." She pointed back and forth from Natalie to JoJo.

"Natalie, you mind telling me what's going on?" Boot asked of his firstborn. "Why these men at my damn house? And I want a straight answer. Like right now! No more bullshitting!"

Mickey felt the need to speak out.

"Pardon me, sir. I wanna apologize if we had caused you any inconvenience by showing up at your home on such a short notice. But I know it's always best that a man be a man and go to the father of the girl he's interested in, to at least have a conversation about having the hand of a daughter. Hopefully, this may be something we can talk about," Mickey proposed.

Martha Jean already had Natalie to pack all her belongings. The decision was made with her. The parents had hoped she'd find a man and get the hell on. Then along came Johnny Mack.

"Boot, Natalie already packed up. We've been waiting on somebody to snatch her from us for the longest. It finally happened. And it wouldn't hurt to let that fella there go ahead and take JoJo off our hands too. We can make more room in the house and be able to save money," she suggested.

Boot stood ramrod. He had both hands on his hips, biting on the inner lining of his jaw, brainstorming over all that was revealed to him.

"You three excuse us men here for a moment. We need some privacy to talk," said Boot. He ordered his ladies to go to the backroom until they were done having a conversation.

One Hour Later . . .

The conversation between the three men came to an end. An agreement was reached. An arrangement was made. Boot called the women back to the living room. He was ready to let them know what his decision was.

"Natalie. Josephine. I don't know what to say about you two. But what I can say, y'all got lucky with these two gentlemen here, in my honest opinion. So, JoJo. What I want you to do is, follow your sister's lead. Go on back there, pack your bags, and y'all two go on to live your lives, okay? Your Mama know better than I do. So, I gotta listen to her when it come to you gals on this. These men gave me their word, that the both of you will be married within three months and living a good life with them. And with that, I wish you two nothing but the best. Be sure to come visit when y'all have the chance to. Now y'all get the hell outta my house before I change my mind!" Boot stated.

He parted his lips, frowned his face, then walked to the bedroom with Martha Jean closely behind. She shut the door and locked it. JoJo had Natalie help her pack up. Once completed, they then left the house with their men and happy as ever. The seaport city of Savannah, Georgia, was now their new residence. They loved it.

Chapter 14

Meanwhile . . .

In Philly, there was no doubt about it, Cornelius "Hound" Savage, had learned his way around the city and bonded well with a group of radical, hardcore street hoodlums. They were his type of guys. And they had welcomed him into their circle with open arms, due to how fearless he was, and being someone only potential opposition of his new crew didn't know.

Hound's down South roots empowered him in a major way. Because he had the ability to get out of town and go home any time that he felt like it, and especially so at the completion of a job (a caper or burglary) or if a beef with any other street crew was to get out of hand and people had to die. Hound's crew was into high stakes robberies, kidnapping for ransom, and smash and grab heists on jewelry stores. These notorious thugs had an insatiable appetite for ruthlessness. And they stopped at nothing to have their way.

The idea was to style and model themselves in the same format as that of the Italian mafia. They had knowledge of the New York Mob families, and also the quasi version that owned and operated a swath area of South Philly. They referred to their territory as "Little Italy" also. Much like New York Mobsters had their locale.

This was it. The big score. The largest take that Hound and his eight cohorts ever attempted to pull off. The plot was to hit an armored bank truck that carried two million in cash from the U.S. Treasury in Washington, D.C. to a bank in the urban community in North Philly. Brown versus Board of Education had passed into law three years prior, integrating the nation racially. And many banks petitioned the government for financial packages to help build up the communities with businesses and stimulate the economy from the flow of income. Equity Trust Bank was granted their application, and the money was in progress.

The stick-up team was provided an inside tip from one of the white female employees, Penelope Reinhardt, who worked as a teller. She carried on an active romantic affair with one of the top guys of Hound's boys. His name was Lacy Smith. A slim, smooth-talking, dark-complexioned dude who loved the streets, and was always eager to hit the next lick. He and his die-hard bandits would go to the ends of the earth in search of the next big hit or were willing to die in the line of fire in getting away from the scene of jacking.

Equity Trust was set to receive two million Tuesday morning. *"At ten sharp,"* Penelope Reinhardt advised him. She also let him know that there would be four armed guards in the truck, two in the front and two in the back. One armed guard would be in the bank. The truck was to pull up directly in front of the bank along the curb of the street. Therefore, it was no need to be too sophisticated. *"Point gun! Rob! Then run!"* said Penelope. They only had a ninety-second window to pull it off. Any time after, the cops would be on the scene.

There they sat at 9:45 A.M. in the getaway car, awaiting the armored truck to arrive. It was Hound, Lacy, Frank, and Russell. They talked briefly until it was time to take action.

"Lacy, you sho' we can take your girl on her word? That these muthafuckas' gonna be here directly at ten, right?" Hound asked.

"Yeah, man! I trust my snow bunny with my life. You know if I take her word that it's safe to come by her house because her parents gone to the boardwalk in Atlantic City, and we could be together all weekend at their house, that I take her word on this," Lacy responded.

"And it's gonna be two million, right?" asked Frank.

"Two million, nigga! Two muthafuckin' million dollars."

"That mean we can split it four ways. At five hundred thousand apiece," chimed in Russell.

"No! We keep four hundred thousand each. My girl gonna get a hunnid thousand each off us for the tip. That's an even split five ways," Lacy further explained.

"Shit! That's still a good take. It should hold us down until the next score," said Hound.

"Goddamn sure should," Frank co-signed. "And since the goddamn government don't wanna take care of its war veterans like they supposed to, we can get it outta their asses this way like we are now."

"Muthafuckin' right, we can!" Hound agreed.

He and Frank slapped fives.

The time reached 10:00 A.M. Lacy spotted the olive-colored armored truck in his rear view. The car they were in was only ninety feet from the bank's front door, on the opposite side of the street in the one-way direction the traffic was to run.

Lacy jumped to action. "Showtime, boys!" he announced.

Everyone then began to put on ski masks and cocked their pistols.

The truck came to a stop directly in front of the bank. The two guards in the front got out and walked to the back of the truck. They had their service revolvers still inside the holsters. One of them banged on the back door. Once the doors flew open, Hound and crew was already running down on them, catching the officers off guard.

"Give it up, muthafucka!" Lacy ordered.

"Get down on the ground now, or I'll blow your fucking head off!" Hound threatened.

Frank and Russell both had smacked the two ground guards on the head with their heavy metaled weapons and forced them face down on the asphalt. They then yanked the other two from the back of the truck to the pavement, face down as well.

The robbers took their pistols from them, then began to grab the cloth money bags in that instance and passed them to Russell who operated as the runner to and fro towards the car. Hound and Lacy cuffed the guards with their own restraints and kept them compliant while the robbery was going on. The lone security guard inside the bank took notice of what was going on and rushed out to break up the caper. Hound was the last man standing at the back door of the truck and had the last two remaining bags of cash clutched in his grip. He turned and began to make his way back to the car.

Click!

"Freeze! You despicable, low-life worthless piece of shit, you!" demanded the elder black cop.

He had his .32 revolver pinned to the back of Hound's head. Hound stopped in his tracks, dropped the bags, then put his hands up high in surrender.

"Don't you make not one more move!" the guard further demanded.

Boom!

Frank came from the blindside and shot the guy in the back of the head. He slumped to the pavement. His head banged violently in the process. Blood poured forth. He was dead as ever. Frank spotted the guard when he first made a break from the front door of the bank. He'd crept low along the side of the parked cars that lined the street. One of the first rules to war is to leave no soldier behind on the battlefield. Frank kept to protocol.

"Come on, Hound! Let's get the fuck outta here!"

Hound was still somewhat paralyzed from fear of the guard having the drop on him. Frank grabbed one of the money bags, Hound had the other. They then speed walked back to the Oldsmobile, hopped in, and sped off with the money they'd hit for. The job was completed in one minute and fifteen seconds. The best part about it was, there were no witnesses. A clean getaway.

Chapter 15

Three Days Later . . .

The four stick-up men divided the take and went their separate ways, Hound bought himself a brand-new car. It was a Lincoln, one that had suicide doors to it. He proved smart about how he put away his money. The rent to the apartment where he lived was paid in advance for one year. His girlfriend at the time, a young twenty-year-old by the name of Precious Williams, stayed over with him most nights. He gave her forty thousand of the money to put away for him. In addition, Hound took a hundred fifty thousand, wrapped it neatly and tight in brown paper bags and plastic, then stashed it away in a secret compartment inside his apartment while alone.

His plan was to drive home to Georgia for a few weeks in his new car until he knew for sure there was no heat from the police. A cop had his brains blown out trying to protect government money, and that didn't go over too well with the mayor of the city, the chief of police, or the feds. The streets were on fire with cops on patrol during investigations, and

Hound did the smart thing, getting the hell on for the time being.

***

Once back in Savannah, he made it his business to get with his two favorite cousins—Johnny Mack and Mickey. He stopped by Mickey's house first. Mickey's Cadillac was parked out front. He and his young girlfriend were there. The time was 4:00 P.M. Hound tapped on the door.

"Mickey! Where you at, cuz? It's me, Hound."

Mickey opened the door.

"Hound! What's up, cuz? How you been, boy?"

The two embraced tightly. They were happy to see one another.

"Who clean car that is you driving? It's brand new too, ain't it?" asked Mickey.

"This my car. I'm the first one to own it. Brand spankin' new."

"Whaaaat! You don't say. Let me have a look at this thing," Mickey responded, then walked to the car to touch and have a closer look.

Mickey had an infatuation with luxury cars. The three things he loved most was money, women, and cars. Clothes came fourth on the list. He opened the door and took a seat behind the wheel. The freshness of the new leather appealed to his senses.

"See now, Hound, you got me wanting to go buy a new car now. I'm jealous of you. In a good way," Mickey said with a smile.

Hound returned one of his own. They then went into the house. JoJo appeared from the back room. She approached Mickey and they kissed.

"Hound, this my new sweetheart here. Her name Josephine. But we call her JoJo for short."

"Hey, JoJo! Nice to meet you. I'm Cornelius. Mickey's cousin. But call me Hound. Everybody do," he greeted. "And welcome to the Savage family as well."

"Hello, Hound! Nice to meet you too. And it's a pleasure to be a part of this family. I'm lovin' it," JoJo respond in her signature sultry tone of voice.

Mickey picked up on something in the way JoJo said the word "pleasure." The way she enunciated was very similar to another female whom JoJo loved. A friend and business associate of his, the sensational Shugg Tatum.

"Oh, yeah. Your favorite lady told me to tell you hello, and for you to get in touch with her the first opportunity you have. You know she crazy about you," Mickey said.

"You must be talking about my Shugg Tatum?" Hound asked. He now smiled wildly.

The mention of Shugg's name excited JoJo. She thought back to the night her and Natalie met the singer at the Chickasaw in the office. The memory of Hound's name being spoken by Shugg came to mind.

"Oh, you the one Shugg asked about!" JoJo let out ecstatically.

She looked from one to the other, from Hound to Mickey then back again, awaiting a reply.

Hound smiled. "You must had her meet Shugg already, Mickey?"

"Hell yeah. She and her sister ain't stopped talking about that night since. That was almost three months ago. The sister Johnny Mack's ol' lady."

"Oh, she is?"

"Mm-hmm! They live together too," Mickey informed.

"That's good, that's good. But look, where your phone at? I'mma give Shugg a call and let her know I'm in town, back in Georgia. I know she may wanna hook up. By the way, how the club doing?"

"It's still up and rolling. We can really get it going if you get Shugg to come perform there again. How soon can she get here from Atlanta?" Mickey asked.

"Maaan! You know Shugg skip to the tune of my words. If I tell her to get here ass here tonight, she's gonna do that," Hound said, then pulled out his wallet to retrieve a list of phone numbers he had.

"You got a direct number to Miss Shugg Tatum?" JoJo asked shyly. She was star-struck over her again.

"Yeah, I do," Hound responded with a smile. "You wanna meet her again? I can have her seated right here in your living room talking with you this weekend."

"Ooh, woo! That'll be amazing! Make that happen, please. I'll do anything to have her visit *my* house," JoJo expressed.

The young girlish giddy side to her came to life in that instance. Both Mickey and Hound had to smile and chuckle at her reaction.

"I'mma make that happen for you, JoJo. I'm about to get her on the phone now," Hound said, dialing the number at the same time.

Mickey and JoJo allowed him a moment of privacy to talk. They returned to the bedroom.

Hound was able to have a long-awaited conversation with Shugg. She promised that she'd be there in Savannah first thing the next morning. She would drive herself in her new Cadillac and make a special appearance at the Chickasaw, but not perform. It was too short of a notice. Shugg only wanted Mickey and Hound to provide her with a couple of security men to protect her. She was too famously known to be by herself, even with the chrome pistol she possessed. Hound gave his word he would and told her to hurry up and get there to him because he was ready to fuck and only desired her love! She felt the same. Once the call was completed, Hound and Mickey hopped into the Lincoln and took a ride to meet up with Johnny Mack and the rest of the Savage family.

While the three of them were together en route to meet others, Hound let them know all about the armored truck lick that he and the crew pulled off. He also let them know he traveled with a hundred thousand and wanted them to put their money together to expand the businesses of the Savage family empire. Since the Chickasaw was doing steady numbers, they would begin with that first. From there, they would buy more land, more houses, and create more start-ups to help employ the many jobless family members they had.

In addition, their intent was to beef up the production and output of all they had going on in the underworld. Heavily supply the liquor houses and increase the purchase of the cocaine and weed they dabbled in was part of the plan as well. The Savage boys had a lot of motion. Their hustle was incredible.

Chapter 16

The Next Day . . .

As promised, Shugg was there in Savannah to be with her lover man, Hound Savage. She crazed over his love making skills and the companionship he provided. They were at the hotel together, one of the poshest establishments near the Savannah River, a popular tourist location. The time was just after 3:00 P.M. and they'd been fucking nonstop from the moment they checked into the suite that morning.

Hound came out of the bathroom. He was asshole naked. Shugg sat atop the bed with her back against the headboard and the cover pulled up just past her breasts. She looked at Hound and marveled at how toned his body was. His dark, satin-smooth skin always triggered her sensual side and stimulated her to a great degree. Her eyes were illuminated with lust, and she smiled wildly. Hound's eleven-inch manhood dangled enticingly between his legs. Shugg wanted more of it, even after having three orgasms of her own to his two.

"What, Shugg?" he asked playfully. He knew what was on her mind.

"You know what. Why you acting like you don't?"

"You want me to put it on you again?"

"Yes, I do. And again and again and again. I could never have too much of you, Cornelius Savage. I fell in love with you the moment we locked eyes and began talking. And I don't know why we keep lollygagging around with one another and not trying to marry and make babies. That's what respectable folks doing nowadays and time. So why you keep holding back on me?" she asked.

Hound now climbed back atop the bed.

"Kids. I might be ready for at some point soon. But marriage. I'm not. And since we on the subject of babies. You still taking those birth control pills, ain't you?" he asked.

Shugg pouted in a disappointed girl type of way.

"I might still be taking them. Or I might not be. Who's to say? I'm ready to have a baby though, Cornelius. So how long I've gotta wait to have you wanting what I want?"

"I don't know, Shugg. I can't say. My black ass too busy out here in these streets ripping and running, to focus on raising some young'uns right now. Just be patient. We gonna get there. Okay?"

"I'm thirty-three years old, Cornelius. I'm not getting any younger. Be sure to keep that in mind."

"I'm aware you're older than I am, Shugg. No need to remind me, sweetheart."

"I mentioned that for a reason. I was really expressing the burning desire I have. It's an older woman's dream to be wanted by a young man and eventually give him a kid. You just a different breed. But I'm hopeful you'll come around at some point or another. Now come on and fuck me some more. *Do me no wrong, baby!*"

She caused Hound to smile by hitting a high note in wording the name of one of her hit songs. That was the one JoJo and Natalie loved so much.

"Shugg, if we keep going like this, we gonna be out of energy and not be able to do a special appearance at the Chickasaw. And besides, my cousins Mickey and Johnny Mack got two lovely young girls who wanna meet you again. And we gonna take y'all to the beach tomorrow. You okay with that?"

She looked and smiled at Hound.

"That damn Mickey and Johnny Mack something else, I tell you. They still got those lil girls with them? Everything must've worked out between them. But yeah. I'm okay with that. I ain't got no problem spending a little more time with them. They was good company last time. Your black ass just need to keep in mind what I said and think about me for a change. That's what I want you to do. I jump when you say jump. I move when you say move. And I came when you said to come. The least you can do is think about me, Cornelius. Is that asking too much?"

Hound paused for a few seconds. They gazed into one another's eyes deeply. He offered her a response.

"Nah. That's not asking too much, Shugg. I'll keep you in mind."

They kissed.

"Now let's get some rest. My ass tired. Shall we?" Hound suggested.

They kissed once more then lay to rest up for the plan they had in mind to do.

***

As agreed upon, Shugg made a special appearance. The next day, Hound took her to Mickey's place as promised to JoJo. Natalie and Johnny Mack were already there. It was late August, and the weather was perfect to make it a good

Sunday on the beach. The three ladies had the opportunity to talk there in JoJo's living room. She and Natalie could not believe it. Just a few months before the day, they were only starstruck fans and idolized the singer. And now, they had direct contact with her and began building a friendship. Not to mention that they were about to go to the beach with her. Now how much of a dream come true was that for the two Bridges siblings, JoJo and Natalie had it good.

Chapter 17

Keeping true to his word with Boot, Mickey married JoJo like he said he would. He had no choice but to have done so. Within the same week of moving her out her parent's home and into his, Mickey released himself inside her womb, running the risk of getting her pregnant. At some point after tying the knot, JoJo did conceive. She now carried and was due to give birth six months from the day.

Because of the fact that JoJo was only sixteen at the time the marriage took place, Mickey was clever enough to utilize the connection to Bobby Kavanaugh and handle the business that he wanted taken care of. Bobby had a niece who clerked at the courthouse in Downtown Savannah. She was paid a pretty penny by Mickey to doctor the documents in forgery to show that JoJo was "eighteen," when in fact she wasn't. Everything worked out well for Ol' Mickey Savage. This was until the unfortunate day when trouble came knocking at his front door. Literally so.

Months Later . . .

". . . Muthafucka'! Y'all tryna break in on me and my wife to rob or kill me! I got you first though, didn't I? And who sent you? I don't owe Dixie! Not a goddamn thing!" Mickey spat.

He was referring to the *Dixie Mafia* of Georgia, once he took notice that the intruders were white.

"You goddamn son of a bitch! I'm a policeman. You shot me and my partner," Flaherty painstakingly let out.

Flaherty then turned his head to the left while now sprawled out on the floor. The lieutenant took notice of the still eyes of the sergeant, the motionless body, and the hole in the forehead of the sidekick. It was the size of a nickel. JoJo rushed into the living room.

"Baby! What's going on! Did you get 'em?"

She looked down and recognized that the wounded victims were white. Fear now paralyzed her. JoJo had never been so terrified in all her years of living. She noticed that one of them was obviously dead as a doorknob. And the other, squirming in pain and struggling to breathe.

"Call me a fucking ambulance, you black bastard. Tell them it's Lieutenant Flaherty and his partner Carson. We've been shot."

"JoJo! Go in the back room, call my cousin, and tell him I say get here as quick as he can, okay? Don't say why. And tell him to come by himself. No one else. Now go!" Mickey demanded of his wife.

He kicked the shotgun and the pistol of the two policemen out of reach. He made it his business to frisk them and check for other weapons.

Mickey began to pace back and forth. He brainstormed thoroughly. He had to think of what to do next. He took a look out the window to know whether or not any other cops accompany. There was none. The unmarked car the two rode in was parked down the street and around the block. They'd walked the distance to Mickey's house. Flaherty became agitated behind Mickey not moving fast enough to his liking.

"Nigger! Did you hear me? I said, call a goddamn ambulance and get me some help. I'm dying here," the lieutenant pleaded.

"I wanna know why the hell you two came to my house and broke down my door? That's what I need you to tell me," Mickey said to the badly wounded officer.

"Boy! If you don't get some goddamn help right now, I say . . . I know something. Now you get!" Flaherty barked. He wheezed in pain and coughed up a gob of blood. His wounds were serious. He continued to rant. "And you already got enough problems on your hands with one dead cop. You'll get the chair for sure if the both of us die," Flaherty threatened.

"Not if nobody knows, now, will I? And I asked you a question. Why are you here to begin with?" Mickey retorted.

"Because boy . . . the body of a beautiful Caucasian gal was found down near the river. She was raped and murdered. An eyewitness reported seeing a blue four-door Cadillac leaving the scene. Ain't too many of them floating around here owned by a 'Shine,' now is it? We narrowed things down a bit. Your name and car came up in the investigation. One of our lieutenants mentioned this to us."

"—Pecan Slim! He the only one that I can think of that'll put my name in something like that. That sapsucker still salty at me for whatever his reasons are," Mickey stated in a voice of anger.

"We showed up to question you. And you shot us! For no reason," Flaherty let out.

The pain was becoming too unbearable. He would surely die if he didn't get medical attention. And fast.

"No. I shot you two muthafuckas' because you came barging into my house unannounced. And then, you dressed in plain clothes. But if you came to question me, where the hell is your warrant?"

"—Boy! I don't need no goddamn warrant here in the great state of Georgia to question or arrest your nigger ass about the rape and murder of a white gal! What ail you? Now you go get me some help, damn it. I'm in pain. I'm dying," he wheezed out.

"And guess what? I don't have to have no compassion to help you either. So, I'mma let your white ass lay right there and die. Now be gone, cracka! Die, I say!" Mickey spat in retort at the policeman.

The lieutenant was now in the throes of death. He weaved in and out of consciousness. Life seeped with every trickle of blood that oozed from his wounds. JoJo ran back to the living room. Mickey was re-situating the door to prevent anyone from possibly passing and looking inside the house.

"Johnny Mack say he'll be over right away."

"Okay. Good. Now look. Go back in there and pack a few travel bags for us. We gotta skip town. Get only the valuable stuff we got. Don't worry about nothing else." He gave his wife specific instructions.

"Yes, baby. I'm on it," she responded.

She went to perform her duty.

"Methuselah Savage," Flaherty spoke again. "You better not let me die here, boy. Because I promise, you'll regret it. You, that pregnant wench of yours there, and that cousin of yours, Johnny Mack. Y'all gonna regret it. In the worst way, if I die too," he said to the best of his ability.

"You should've thought about all that shit when you made the decision to break down my goddamn door and forced your way into my house unannounced. It ain't no fun when the rabbit got the gun, now is it!" Mickey taunted.

He then took everything in the policemen possession that could lead back to him and a shooting taking place. The intent was to take the cops and their belongings to some remote location and dump them all together.

Starting with the dead one, Mickey began to strip him out of the clothing he had on, packed them in a paper bag, and prepare to move them. He got to Flaherty, the near-dead one, to do the same. The lieutenant slapped and pawed at Mickey with what little strength he had left. It wasn't much at all to slow the activity of the process.

Mickey came to the conclusion that he'd have a better chance at staying alive and free by him and Johnny Mack simply dumping the bodies, never to be found, than to run the risk of calling the police to report the incident. He'd be shot down in a lead slaughter for sure by any responding police. The only backlash he was subject to face by doing things this way was that he and Johnny Mack would have no choice but to leave Savannah and go north to live for a long time to come. However, this was a move already contemplated upon, being convinced by Hound that the north was the place to be. That they needed to join him there.

The thought came to Mickey as to whether he should or shouldn't contact Bobby Kavanaugh, and let him know of the situation, and get his advice on what best to do. His only hang-up about this was he had no idea on when would be a good time to do so. Whether then and there in the moment, or after the fact, once long gone out the state. Maybe Johnny Mack could help him think over what was best to do.

Chapter 18

Johnny Mack finally arrived. His initial reaction was one he hadn't ever thought would be.

"Mickey! What the hell you got going on, boy?" he exclaimed.

He pinned his hands on top of his head and held his mouth wide open at the sight of the two laid out white men he put eyes on. Mickey gave him a quick rundown on what unfolded and how they got to where they were. He then explained why he specifically called upon him and not the cops or for an ambulance.

In 1958, in the state of Georgia, there was absolutely no reasonable explanation that *any* black man could give as to why two prominent white Savannah Police Detectives had been shot and then have the opportunity to walk away with his freedom still, let alone his life. Whether justifiable or otherwise, it wasn't going to happen.

"Johnny Mack! What do I do? I really don't know. I'm lost," Mickey stated.

"Hell, I don't know either! What the fuck you done got me involved in with you now, Mickey!" Johnny Mack was terrified out of his ever-loving mind. However, not so much to the point of panic. He spoke again. "All I know is we better do something. And fast!"

"Do we take 'em and dump 'em? Or do we wanna leave 'em to be found?" asked Mickey.

"Cuz, I think it'll be best if we have them be gone for good, never to be found. Because if they are, ain't no telling who they already mentioned something to about them coming to get you. He did bring up Pecan Slim, didn't he? So, what we do is put a blaze to the Caddy, once we take these peckerwoods out to the country some place and bury 'em deep in the dirt. Then, we haul ass up North, so the police won't be busy tryna track down everybody who was in your car the night Pecan Slim and the other one pulled us over. End of discussion," Johnny Mack stated.

"Do I contact Kavanaugh, or not?" asked Mickey.

"Who?"

"Kavanaugh. My buddy, Bobby. The guy I had Pecan Slim get in touch with through dispatch at the station. He had them to let us go that night. Remember?"

"Mickey! A goddamn traffic stop is one thing, nigga. But two dead cops who you shot to death? That's another. Now how tight do you really think you and that Kavanaugh guy is? Ask yourself that much, fool!"

"You make a good point. It ain't no way that me and a goddamn *honkey* that close to where he'd overlook an incident like this. Not to mention the fact that he is an Assistant DA. And I'm not even gonna begin to let you know anything about the business relationship we got—me and

Bobby. But in due time, I will though. It don't matter right now."

"Understood, Mickey. That's understood," Johnny Mack responded.

"JoJo!" Mickey called out for his wife again. "Johnny Mack about to take you over to his place. That way you and your sister can have a talk with one another. You gonna help her pack her bags, then y'all gonna get on the train and head north to Philadelphia, okay? And by the time y'all get there, I will have gotten in touch with my people and have them pick y'all up. Me and Johnny Mack gonna be up that way at a later date. Now go on," Mickey further ordered his wife.

His instructions were clear and to the point. He then hugged her and gave her a kiss. She and Johnny Mack took off from there, en route to his place.

**

Lieutenant Flaherty had already taken his last breath. His days on earth were no more. The Grim Reaper came to pay him a visit, one that no man welcomes, at least not the ones in their right minds.

"Son of a bitch!" Mickey yelled at himself.

He was in a fit of panic over the second policeman dying as well. But the intention was to do away with them both anyhow. So, it really didn't matter.

"My black ass gonna get the goddam 'lectric chair twice over now. Once in this life and once in the life that's to come! What the fuck do I do now?" he continued to express in soliloquy.

In Mickey's mind, the situation intensified drastically, in real time. And on a realistic level from the problems that were to come. Mickey panicked in a way. He was subject to make mistakes throughout the process if he failed to keep his composure.

Chapter 19

Four Days Earlier . . .

Norma Elaine Maddox, better known in the modeling industry as "Lady Maddox," performed at a photo shoot for a particular modeling agency that was locally owned in the Savannah area. Her specialty was swimwear, two-piece suits that revealed an abundant amount of skin and figure.

The agency's owner was a member of a well-established family. They owned real estate, furniture, car dealerships, and other businesses dotted about the city. The modeling gig was a way for the young owner to utilize "Sparkling Stars" to develop friendships with young females and socialize from time-to-time. It was also to offer aspiring models the opportunity to make a name for themselves and to grace the pages of the fashion and up and coming celebrity magazines. Lady Maddox was all for it.

The agency owner and Lady Maddox met three weeks before the day. An agreement was reached to do business. In her efforts to further convince the owner that she had all the qualities and talent necessary to push her past the competition, she offered to do private shoots where she could pose either topless or full nude. Smut magazines were on the rise at the time and held popular acclaim. The bottom line was that she was willing to do whatever to gain his attention to advance her career, so long as the requirement wasn't of an actual intercourse nature. She knew from past bad experiences that it wasn't good to mix business and pleasure, no matter what the profession.

Lady Maddox had a serious problem on her hands. She didn't know that the agency owner was a spoiled brat and hailed from a family that had power and ability to get him out of any trouble he might find himself in. He felt he could do whatever the hell he wanted. And there wasn't a damn thing anyone could do about it, because he had an uncle who was a member of the judicial community, and a father who had money and power. Basically, he was a highly privileged young white male in America. So, upon signing Lady Maddox to the company like a few females before her, the owner felt entitled to her body how he saw fit, sexually or otherwise, and wouldn't be snubbed or denied any type of way. It'd be over his dead body before he would.

On this particular Friday, the agency owner, along with Jeremy, a close friend, picked up Lady Maddox from the hotel she'd been staying in, for them to travel out to the beach on Tybee Island to do a private photo shoot. This would be the second of this style of manner. But one "exclusively for her," according to the words of the owner. He erected a small tent that had the capability to cover its sides. Just prior to sunset, the owner wanted her to pose in the nude. He'd hired a photographer to specifically accommodate them for the occasion. He wanted to impress Lady Maddox and make her feel appreciated, as no one before him had treated her in this type of way.

The problem was the owner had become extremely infatuated with Lady Maddox and stalked her for the weeks leading up to this day. He was dangerously in love but had no ability to have her like he desired. This became the thing to make matters worse, being refused.

It wasn't that the owner didn't have the material possessions necessary to attract a female. That wasn't the issue. The problem was he didn't have the physical attributes to make females look at him that way, nor the articulation to please them with words. He was a polar-bear-type husky dude, not to mention, impolite, obnoxious, arrogant to the umpteenth degree, and very cynical. He had it in his mind that money and material possessions could get him sex when he wanted, but that proved to be a difficult task with Lady Maddox. She wasn't buying what he was selling. No amount of money could he offer to make her see him in that way, lay atop her, and penetrate her precious womb with the pork sausage like penis he had.

They completed the photo shoot. The sun had just set. It was time to leave for the day. The two had built up enough trust to where he could now pick her up and drop her off. The owner paid Lady Maddox and the photographer. Jeremy also acted as his driver from time to time, so his pay was weekly. The owner and Lady Maddox rode in the backseat alongside one another. He had a few things of a "business nature" he needed to discuss with her, so he said.

While on the highway headed back to the city, the owner began to aggressively grope on Lady Maddox in the rear of his new modeled Cadillac. It was brown in color, a Fleetwood. He previously owned a blue one, same make and model, only older. It was sold to a business partner of his uncle's. The guy who bought the car was also a friend of the family, a black guy. He'd helped their family earn a pretty penny as well throughout the underworld. He benefited them in many ways.

On more than one occasion, the agency owner, the black friend of the family, and Jeremy, had loaded and unloaded cargo of illegal contraband on the bank of the Savannah River. The owner's family owned illegal moonshine distilleries in the wilderness and marshland of Chatham County and up the river in South Carolina. So, there were only a few who knew about this particular location, the loading spot that they utilized. This area would play a crucial role in their lives beginning that day.

The more and more the modeling agency owner attempted to sweet talk the tender Lady Maddox and grope her against her will the more she resented him. She then put up a fight to fend him away, further adding insult to injury upon the ego and sexual impulse of the owner with the snub. He forced himself atop of her.

"Get off of me! Get away you fat, sweaty, disrespectful bastard!" she yelled at him.

Her physical strength wasn't enough to fight him off. Her screams went to no avail in the backseat of the moving vehicle. The owner lost total control of himself from that point. His infatuation and sexual craze for her pushed him on. He grabbed Lady Maddox around the throat with both hands to subdue and overpower her. He then ripped her thin material garment in half in his effort to get her naked. Her panties followed.

While holding her down onto the seat with one hand, he used his other to loosen the drawstring of his swim trunks and pushed them down to his knees. His erect penis was now exposed. The owner then continued imposing his will upon the model, choking her and now penetrating her at the same time. Lady Maddox clawed at him, cutting his flesh with her bright painted nails in a few areas. She bit him on his meaty chest. He became more aggressive. He locked both hands around her throat then squeezed mercilessly. His heavy torso had her pinned to the seat and he thrust away, carrying out his barbaric carnal act of rape he was now fully engaged in.

In the owner's mind, the only way he planned to stop in his attack was if one of two scenarios happened first—he would ejaculate and release his load in her—or he would continue to choke her until she was rendered unconscious and no longer breathing. In this strange coincidental instance, both occurred at the same time. Lady Maddox had been killed that very moment he exploded his diabolical load inside of her.

There became an even more sickening part to it. The owner had his friend drive down to the bank of the river to the area they knew well. Once there, Jeremy now had the leeway to ram his *peckerwood* inside of her how he saw fit. The owner insisted that he did so, totally disregarding the fact that the teenage girl was now dead. At that point, they ripped the remainder of her clothing from her body, then dragged her naked body out the car and down to the edge of the water. The two then departed the scene.

***

Shortly after that night, the agency owner made anonymous phone calls to make a report. He was now aiming to frame someone.

Anyone would do, he thought. "I know just who," he said to Jeremy. "That nigger, Mickey Savage! He could easily take the fall for this."

And so, the majority of what was reported implicated the car and identity an innocent man owned. Someone who had done no such thing. The report first went by the ears of one Jimmy Wilkens aka "Pecan Slim," the Savannah police lieutenant. He had knowledge of the subject who the caller mentioned by name. He also knew the car, the blue Cadillac Fleetwood with the tail fin rear end.

The domino effect began to fall how they may against Mickey Savage. And then, enter the two cops, breaking down the door to his place, leading him to shoot them on instinct. His luck couldn't have been any worse. The shooting and killing of two white policemen in Georgia in 1958, by a black man, was something absolutely not thought of. Now how ugly of a situation was that for him?

Mickey now found himself in a scenario where he was in a triangle of trouble that had one way in, and no way out. That was definitely not a good predicament to be in. Not at all.

Part Two

Making Power Moves

Chapter 20

Five Years Later . . .

In relocating to the north and eventually settling in the city of "Brotherly Love," Philadelphia, PA, Mickey and Johnny Mack managed to adjust well from the night that they fled Savannah. They took the bodies of Lieutenant Flaherty and Sergeant Carson and buried them in a cornfield in the rural area of the country. Mickey then had no choice but to set his gleaming Cadillac ablaze during the trip up north. He torched it in South Carolina, then got into the car with Johnny Mack to continue the journey.

Mickey and Johnny Mack sold the Chickasaw to a set of suitable buyers. It was another powerful black family in

Savannah, who was making a rise in the underworld, the Solomon family. They paid good money for the club. The money the Savages had was used to help them establish themselves in both a legit way and an illegitimate one. A totally new life had to be made.

At the time, the police had put out numerous missing persons reports of the two cops who'd been killed. However, that served to no avail, and no one called in to report having seen either of the two. The unmarked car they'd driven to the area where Mickey's house was located was later stolen the day after the fact and stripped of all the parts that could be sold individually. It was Flaherty's personal car. The investigation of their disappearance became complicated. It went cold.

Johnny Mack and Natalie relocated across the bridge from Philly in Camden, New Jersey. Mickey and Josephine remained rooted in the city. He situated JoJo in a decent four-bedroom home in Northeast Philly just off Frankfurt Avenue. They needed a place to accommodate them and the four kids they now had. Another was on the way. In the five-year time span, the Savages had added to the family in a significant way. Johnny Mack and Natalie had two of their own as well. For one—Johnny Mack—he was done with making babies. Two was enough. But for the other Savage—Mickey—he wasn't quite to that conclusion just yet. Mickey was madly in love with JoJo's sweet honey hole. The pleasure he received from the soul controller she had between her legs was unmatched by anything else he'd ever experienced. He'd always felt that way from the very first time he had the opportunity to sex her.

Due to the legal implications Mickey could potentially face in the South if his name was run through the system, there was no way he was able to apply for a legitimate job in the workforce. He feared a possible warrant might have been issued for his arrest. Therefore, he settled on being his own man like he had been all along, and doing what he did in the underworld to earn money to take care of his family. Mickey was a hustler and a jack of all trades in the streets. He and Johnny Mack made the business connections and got into the world of running numbers in the hood, operating gambling houses, whore houses where they had madams overseeing and assisting them, and speakeasies where alcohol was sold. No matter what the odds were against them, they had to get it how they live. And they had no problem with that. Mickey fully embraced the street life. He elevated his level of finesse to the highest potential.

JoJo, on the other hand, did enjoy the life she now had with her husband. But also, resented it in a way, due to Mickey keeping her pregnant and barefoot, and not being able to go and come how she saw fit. Only across the Delaware River to her sister Natalie's house, the grocery store, the department store, and to the local drug store, that was basically about it for JoJo. She learned to adjust and not complicate things for Mickey any more than they already were, being that she knew first-hand about the killing of those two cops. Besides, her kids preoccupied her in a good way. There was Mary, Martha, Jacob and Ishmael, in that order, and she adored them.

Through the summer months leading through the years to 1963, JoJo had help with the kids from one of her younger siblings, Sasha. Mickey would pay travel fees for her to come and spend time with them. She would also go to Natalie's house to help her too. But the focus was on JoJo and her four.

***

In addition to Mickey keeping contact with family down in Georgia, he also maintained a steady connection with possibly his best working girl and good friend, a female better known as "Miss Peaches." Mickey had her at his command for quite a while. She was his most valuable companion. Without Miss Peaches, Mickey was unable to turn Bobby Kavanaugh like a thumbscrew. He couldn't have worked him as he had for the years that he'd been able to do so. Bobby was obsessed with the brown-skinned sultry sensation that Miss Peaches proved to be. She was his mistress and accompanied him on many occasions.

Miss Peaches advised Mickey that there was no legal trouble to worry about down in Savannah. And that Bobby sends his best regards to his friend on his new life out in "California." Although Mickey and Bobby did have communication with each other through the years, Mickey dared not let him know exactly where he now lived. But instead, he lied and told his prosecutor friend he had better opportunities in the Golden State than he and his young wife experienced in the Peach State. Bobby didn't question too much, and Mickey didn't reveal too much. Their business now was Miss Peaches and strictly her alone.

Mickey had a new agenda in his mind. He needed Miss Peaches' help to achieve this feat. In a phone conversation the two had, he told her what he had in motion, and for her to get there to Philly at the first available opportunity. They hadn't seen one another physically in the years he'd been away, only in the pictures they'd exchanged through the mail. And they were eager to meet. It would be a long time coming. Miss Peaches agreed to travel. He wired her the money to do so. Not that she needed it, because Bobby kept her flush with cash. Mickey simply felt the need to do so.

Chapter 21

Miss Peaches was now in Philly in Mickey's presence, at the 30th Street train station. He drove to pick her up and was in the process of taking her to a hotel to settle in. Once there, they continued in conversation to somewhat catch up on things. He let her specifically know that he mainly needed her to "cultivate" the men of influence he was looking to curry favor with. And if anybody, she would definitely be the one more suited in this regard. The conversation then shifted to the affair she carried on with Bobby Kavanaugh.

Miss Peaches was now twenty-six years of age, but still looked the part of the twenty-one-year-old she was when Mickey last laid eyes on her. Her height was still five-six, and she maintained her weight at a hundred twenty-five pounds. Her skin was dark as soot but smooth as the most exclusive silk garment. She had a wasp-like waistline and a flat belly due to her daily routine practice of wearing a laced corset. *My body is my product, and I must keep the buying customer happy, and continue to be pleasing to the eyes*, she would often think.

Miss Peaches loved to boast in good nature about her figure. Those cantaloupe-sized juicy breasts of hers always enticed the eyes of those who were spellbound over her beauty. There had been a lot of money, time, and discipline put into her body as she was determined to keep it that way for the satisfaction of her clientele. Mickey now had the duty to acquaint the two women in his life with one another. Once Miss Peaches had put her belongings away and showered, Mickey returned to pick her up and they went to his home for her to meet JoJo.

"Peaches, meet my wife here. Her name is Josephine, but JoJo for short," Mickey introduced. "And JoJo, meet Evelyn Ayton. Miss Peaches."

Miss Peaches stepped forward to greet and shake JoJo's hand. She was dressed in a dark blue form-fitting dress and heeled in a pair of expensive D'Orsay pumps. Her demeanor was always confident with a slight touch of arrogance. JoJo instantly felt some type of way about the beautiful and sexy female, who had features of Dravidian Indian ancestry, having access to her husband. Not to mention, just now being made aware of it.

"Your wife, you say, Mickey. You don't say. Nice to meet you, Miss Mickey Savage. I'm sure you're aware of how lucky you are to have a man like him," she said.

The two females continued to look at one another, sizing up their demeanor and approach. JoJo returned the same energy and tone.

"Honestly, Miss Peaches, I take all you just said with a grain of salt and a smile. And it's nice to meet you too." She then looked towards her husband. "But the question remains, Methuselah Savage. Why am I just now being made known of a woman—it appears—who may know more about you than I do? That's what I'd like to know."

"*Knew* me longer than you? Yes. That's true. But *knows* me more than you? No. And to be clear, me and Peaches are only friends. For business purposes," he responded, providing clarity.

He felt like he needed to let JoJo know exactly what type of relationship he and Miss Peaches shared.

"Mind if I ask where you from, Peaches?"

"I don't mind at all. Originally, I'm from the Bahamas, the capital city of Nassau. But I moved to Savannah at an early age. If that's to answer your question well enough for you."

"Oh! Interesting now. You lived in Savannah, I see."

"That be correct. And you?"

Mickey took a relaxing position on the couch and allowed the two women to exchange subtle digs at one another. The feline pleasantries shot back and forth humored him in a way. He had nothing to do at the moment. It was just past dark. The kids were upstairs in bed watching TV, and the three adults were getting familiar with one another and entertaining all together.

"I was born and raised in Eatonton, Georgia."

"Where? I never heard of that place."

"Eatonton. It's not too far from Savannah."

Oh. But I never heard of it."

"And how did you and my Mickey meet?"

"It's a long story, little lady."

"We definitely have the time. Please relate." Miss Peaches took a hard look at Mickey. She had a smirk streaked across her face. She then put her attention back to JoJo.

"How do you like your drinks, JoJo? Straight or chased?"

"When I ain't pregnant, I prefer it straight. So gimme what you got," JoJo retorted in a stern way. "Pretend I ain't pregnant now."

Miss Peaches turned to have a look at Mickey once more, basically for permission to proceed. He shrugged his shoulders, indicating for her to do so. She held back no longer.

"Listen, baby girl. Okay, I sell pussy for Mickey here. And been doing so since the age of sixteen. That's ten years now. He and I have a mutual understanding that supersedes anything related to a boyfriend-girlfriend thing. We're better than that. It's business over pleasure. And there ain't no playtime in between. You understand now?" Miss Peaches stated emphatically.

"So, it's business over pleasure with you two, huh?"

"Yes. At this point now. And if you want to know have I ever had him sexually? Let's just say, Mickey means well. And we'll leave it at that. Shall we. Miss Savage?"

"And that, we shall do," Mickey chimed in to say. He'd heard enough. "Look JoJo. This what we got going on, okay? Peaches is here on business. She's with us. With you and me. And at times, she gonna be staying under the same roof as us. Here. With me, you, and the kids. And there's nothing to argue or debate. Eventually, she'll be getting a place of her own to live. So, between the time, it's here, the hotel . . . hotel . . . here. Okay?"

Mickey laid down the law how he wanted things done under his roof. There was no pushback or challenge from JoJo. His opportunity to increase influence and money throughout the Philly underworld became greater. He already had a few irons in the fire, but was making nowhere near the money he was now set to draw in. And that was millions to be earned, a number he'd yet to reach.

JoJo had one last thing she wanted to remind Mickey of before they concluded with the discussion.

"Mickey. Look. Okay. You know ever since you took me in with you and out from under my daddy's roof, I have completely obeyed your every command, right?"

"Right. You have, baby," he responded.

"And no doubt about it, I plan to keep it that way. Because I'm a Christian woman, and a country girl who has Southern pride and values. I'm your wife. You're my husband. And you have the leeway to do all you so please. Because you're the one who takes care of everything like a man supposed to. You can do me no wrong," she said, causing Mickey to smile in delight behind the phrase, being he knew JoJo got it from Shugg Tatum, the singer she loved so much.

"—Where we going with this, JoJo?" He urged her to get to the point. "Because you already know, we're gonna stay above feeling and emotions to the best of our ability. You have me. That's all to matter. I need Peaches' help business-wise."

"Okay. You're right. Just keep in mind, I had your four kids. We've got another on the way. And on top of that, we're in this together. We have everything to gain and everything to lose . . . together. Whether we want to be, or we don't. Just continue to be mindful. That's all I ask," she capped off, maintaining strong eye contact.

The thing JoJo was hinting at was about the situation with the two cops having been killed she had direct knowledge of. And that he had the incident hanging over his head. At any time, if he was to get all the way out of line, she'd definitely bring him back to reality with the thought of it.

JoJo then walked away from him, leaving her husband with a lot to think over. Mickey and Miss Peaches had business to get to. They left the house to go attend to such.

Chapter 22

Hound Savage had recently been released from state prison he'd been locked up for the past three years. He had to go do a bid behind a jewelry store smash and grab heist not turning out so well. Hound was one of the two men who had gotten captured in the process, leaving him to be sent away on a conviction of robbery by force.

Hound had no choice but to put his trust and reliance on his girlfriend at the moment, Precious Williams. They had an apartment together. And she'd been there with him throughout the many times he and his goons went on licks and hit capers. Hound left her with the money, the jewels, and all the other valuable materials that he'd gained in those robberies. A bad move. She'd run off on him at the very onset of the sentence he had to serve. And now he was out, with her on the list of people to be dealt with at the very instance he laid eyes on her.

Hound made valuable connections while in prison and looked to capitalize upon them in free society. He also reconnected to his old buddies, Frank, Lacy and Russell, and they all had ambitions to rise in the streets again. And now that his two favorite cousins were in Philly to live, Hound looked to have an explosive rise to power along with them. One like they'd never experienced before. Thus, the birth of the original Black Mafia Family began to form and take shape at its core there in the North Philly ghetto.

The three Savage boys had the money to put together a successful enterprise of some sort and were looking to make an investment in a product that would put them over the top in the underworld. At the time, heroin was king. And the streets craved it in a major way. The only people who had product was the Italian Mafia. They had a direct line to the French Connection and the product they controlled was so potent and so powerful that it could be cut two to three times, and still hold a great deal of quality.

But herein lay the problem: the Italian mob didn't do business directly if at all with the blacks, and were very reluctant to do so, even with a third party in place. However, word got to Hound that the don of the Marconi Crime Family in South Philly—Angelo Marconi—had no problem opening the door and doing business with "suitable black distributors," in his words, if they proved to be of benefit and a profit to him and his family. Not to mention, certain aspects of black culture and customs Don Angelo took favor with, especially in sports. Boxing topped the chart. Black Philly fighters were on the rise and Don Angelo wanted a stake in their success. Hound had an Italian guy he'd linked with in prison. A guy named Rocco Brunelleschi. They had plans to do business once free. The moment was at hand.

Rocco was a made man in the Marconi Family. He and his brother Anthony, Tony for short. Hound contacted Rocco and let him know that he and his two cousins were ready to do business. Rocco told him to report to his pool room in

Little Italy in South Philly, to make a deal. Hound, Mickey, and Johnny Mack made the drive to the south side of the city with the bread in tow they were looking to spend and get off on a good foot in the game. All three looked the part and were properly dressed in business attire. Mickey, the polished of the three, was sure to require this of them. He was the apparent leader, and in his mind, he wouldn't have it any other way.

Once there at the location, they were met by Rocco, the capo of the crew Joey, Tony, Don Angelo's nephew, Little Alley Boy, and Sammy "The Horse." The mobsters had on common street gear they wore almost daily—sweatsuits, and baseball caps. Mickey and company were escorted through the front portion of the billiards to the backroom. There was a table and chairs for them to have a seat. They were frisked first, then allowed to sit.

"Nice to meet you, gentlemen," the capo Joey said. "No secret why we're here. So, let's cut through the chase and get straight to the business, shall we?"

"That we shall do," Mickey responded, putting himself at the forefront as being the designated leader. Neither Hound nor Johnny Mack objected to Mickey's words or perception.

"And you are?" Joey asked.

"I'm Mickey. Mickey Savage. The cousin of Hound here. I speak for us all."

The two men shook hands. Everyone else followed their lead.

"Rocco tells me you guys are looking to do a little business! Smack tends to be a huge money maker in the world nowadays. And the Marconi Family would like to have some of it by supplying nothing but the best. How much you guys looking to spend?"

"We got about two hundred thousand to begin with. The more business we do, the more we spend on future deals. How much product does that type of money get us?" Mickey asked.

Joey snapped his fingers to signal for his doorman to bring the goods. The guy disappeared then returned two minutes later. He passed Joey the mini military duffle bag he had clutched in his hand. One-by-one, Joey sat each kilo of heroin on the table. There were twenty in total.

Joey spoke up again. "Twenty kilos here for the two hundred thousand you fellas looking to spend. They sell ten thousand each. Nothing but the best around at the moment," he related.

Mickey and his cousins took a look at the bricks and all nodded heads in agreement that Joey offered a good deal. There was no need for them to check the product to know if it was real or not. It went without saying. The Italian mobsters had more to lose by trying to sell someone fake material, than simply doing straight-up business, and they couldn't afford to play those types of games. Besides, they knew they had a set of bona fide customers in the Savage boys and wanted all the business that they came to them with.

"You have a deal. We want 'em," Mickey said, then opened the nylon material bag he had and sat the money on the table. "It's all there. No need to count it," he stated.

Joey took the money and handed it to the elder mobster present with them. He and Mickey shook hands.

"I hope to see you guys again soon," Joey said.

"No doubt, you will. A lot. If the product be all that like you say it is," Mickey responded.

He and Joey smiled at one another. The business between the two went exceptionally well. The Savage boys then left the back room with their product and headed to the car. They went to Hound's apartment in North Philly to break down the product and package it up for retail. The particular neighborhood where Hound lived would be the prime territory for them to take over and move narcotics they now had. They were in the "Bad Lands," a notorious and ruthless turf any day of the week.

Chapter 23

Two Months Later . . .

On November 22, 1963, two particular incidents took place that would forever be etched in the memory of Mickey and JoJo. The first was the fact of JoJo giving birth to the fifth child, a son. They named him Isaac. And the second, was the assassination of the 35th President of the United States, John Fitzgerald Kennedy.

JoJo dropped her load ironically about seven minutes before the first reports of shots being fired. The alleged killer was Lee Harvey Oswald. As Mickey and his wife rejoiced in their son being welcomed into the world, the nation recoiled behind the news of the president's death and began to mourn the passing of a good man and great leader. The couple now had two daughters and three sons. A bigger home was needed.

***

At the point when it became a necessary time to kill, Hound and his designated henchmen, were the ones who would track down those marked for death and then put them away. Bad apples and outside threats always popped up and putting them down would be a mandatory duty. Hound had no problem doing so.

A particular instance occurred where Hound was called upon to do work, he and his pack of bloodthirsty dawgs he ran with. Three people had to go, two females and one male, all behind an elaborate scheme that they'd been working on over Mickey for the better part of the month. There was a lot of counterfeit money circulating in Philly at the time. Lester, one of Mickey's *distros*, knew the producer of the fake bills, and he wanted in on the play.

What Lester would do was, he'd take real money he'd made from drug sales, spend it on the counterfeit, he would receive double the amount of fake cash for what he would pay in real currency. Then he'd take half counterfeit and half real money to buy more product from outside sources by using Mickey and Johnny Mack's names, get rid of the product with the two females he had doing the dirty work with him. He'd buy more counterfeit money, pay Mickey half and half for more kilos of heroin, then repeat all over again without no one knowing a thing because of how well covered up the scheme was, until the truth finally came to the light.

Mickey had gotten a tip from an Italian business associate of his who knew Lester worked for him. The guy related to him that one of the females who worked with Lester utilized Mickey's name to buy two kilos of "boy" from them, and the money wasn't right. Half was real and the other half wasn't. This became a problem and had to be dealt with.

The two females on Lester's team were working girls in the North Philly territory. Miss Peaches was familiar with who they were from the few occasions they'd shown up with Lester to meet Mickey. She trailed them to know exactly where Lester was laying low then let Mickey know. He put Hound on the job.

Hound and two of his goons caught the main female leaving a bar out in West Philly, kidnapped the bitch off the street while she was unlocking the door to her Oldsmobile, and put a beat down on her all the way to North Philly. Once there, they yanked her from the car, took her to the basement of the house, then slammed her hard onto the concrete floor. This was a secondary house owned by Mickey. He and Johnny Mack were there and began to drill her with hardliner questions. She told everything in the hopes that he'd let her walk. That didn't happen.

"Hound! Eat!" Mickey ordered.

The vicious executioner took hold of a claw hammer that was there to serve the purpose. Hound then bashed the female conspirator about the head multiple times, killing her with ease. She was no more. Her body was disposed of, never to be found.

That same night, Hound and his working crew went to the apartment where Lester and the other female were located. They were awaiting the return of the one that had already been tracked down earlier. The hitters then barged into the place with guns drawn, and subdued Lester and the chick. Hound then called Mickey to come to the spot. He arrived shortly thereafter.

"Terminate these two greedy muthafuckas,' Hound!"

Hound allowed his two bloodthirsty goons the opportunity to quench their appetite for blood by whacking one each. Mickey then took everything of value Lester had on hand. The heroin stash the con man had left was taken too, along with fifty thousand in real money and a hundred thousand in counterfeit. The problem Mickey faced coming from Lester was now put to bed. He'd cut off the head of the thieving snake. The ass of it soon followed.

Chapter 24

Several Months Later . . .

The time lapse between the last chance Mickey and Bobby Kavanaugh had the opportunity to personally meet was five years. A lot of things had changed for both men, as their rise to power came to be. Bobby was now the official District Attorney over the entire judicial circuit. As such, the new position provided tremendous power and an unlimited resource war chest of taxpayer money that stuffed the coffers of the counties he served.

Bobby was elected to the office two years prior and his top priority as a prosecutor was to solve cases and convict guilty people of serious violent offenses. Also, the disappearance of Lieutenant Flaherty and Sergeant Carson, and the unsolved case of Norma Elaine Maddox, being raped and murdered, topped his agenda to bring to a close, due to the polarizing negative effect that those cases held over the public. There was something about those two that stuck with him.

Bobby wanted to meet up with his longtime friend, Mickey, and the female he'd adored for many years, Miss Peaches. This was a good time for Bobby to do so, while on a vacation perhaps, down in Miami, Florida, a destination he was set to travel to. He was a Republican elected official, and the Republican Party had a scheduled gathering in beautiful Miami, for the week leading up to the big heavyweight showdown between the young brash-mouth challenger, Cassius Marcellus Clay, who was looking to shake up the world with a potential defeat of the brute and dominating reigning champion, Sonny Liston. The fight was to be held in Miami. Mickey wanted to attend and also visit with his two eldest children, Rachel and Elijah, who lived there. Bobby wanted the company of Miss Peaches. A perfect scenario for the two men. It was ideal for business and pleasure.

Miss Peaches maintained a continued contact with Bobby. He let her know the idea he had in mind for both of them, that a much needed get away would do them well. His treat. She had no problem with the offer. He'd been under the impression that Miss Peaches was away visiting family in New Orleans, and had no idea she was up north helping Mickey carry out his agenda.

***

The four companions were now down in Miami, enjoying the weather and parlaying on the beach. Miss Peaches brought along a younger recruit of hers to keep Mickey company while she did so with Bobby. The tender female's name was Sparkle Andrews, a sultry nineteen-year-old who was under the attention of the veteran lady of the night. Miss Peaches knew what Mickey's taste and appetite was, and his preference in females. Sparkle would be a good match. As the two ladies sunbathed atop large beach towels, Mickey and Bobby strolled along the beach holding a conversation, catching up on many things in the moment.

"Mickey, I missed you, buddy. And all that good money we use to make together. Where you now living?" he asked him. "You just up and hauled ass on me. Like you had to hurry and get away from something. You know I'm the head DA now. I make all the decisions on any and all criminal cases. The central role and mission of a DA is public safety. I have to keep people safe and maintain that."

"I've been away, Bobby. Living in California now. Got family there as well. Me and my wife had grown tired of Savannah."

"Wanted a change of scenery, huh? I can understand that. Sometimes we all need it. But I'm a good ol' Georgia boy. I was born and raised, hold office, and have a career there, not to mention, the land and businesses the Kavanaugh family own there. Only if I could keep that damn reckless party animal of a nephew of mine in check—Seth—and his head screwed on correctly, our name may not sound so crude to a lot of the good ol' tax paying people of Chatham County. He's gotten to the point where he needs me to make a criminal offense go away at least twice a month. You remember Seth, don't you?"

"Of course I do, Bobby. He and I have made many pick-ups and drop-offs together. For you, to be exact. You know I remember him."

"Oh, that's right. Damn! How could I forget about that? Those floating beauties of ours used to come and go up and down the river with ease, didn't they? Time sure does fly, don't it, Mickey?"

"It definitely does. And remember, Seth was the one who sold me that lovely Cadillac. I really liked that car. Until that damn Pecan Slim Wilkens began to harass me like crazy about it. That son of a gun thought like all hell I had stolen that car. Until I had him get in touch with you one night to verify that it was clean."

"The crazy thing about that night was shortly after, Wilkens, coincidentally contacted me yet again. Something about getting a tip at the station from a caller reporting a blue Cadillac being spotted down near the river at one of our pick-up spots. That was odd to me."

"What was that all about?"

"He said something about two people being in the car at first, but only one when the vehicle left. The caller said it was a black male behind the wheel, and a white female by his side. The body of a young white female by the name of Norma Maddox, was discovered the next day after the call. She'd been raped and strangled to death. A damn shame. But anyway, that particular case, and one that involves two missing law enforcement men of ours, are high on my case load I've got to solve. They're personal to me. It was part of my campaign pledge to put the guilty away behind the killings," Bobby related with a serious tone to his voice.

Chapter 25

Mickey took a minute to process all Bobby made him aware of. He thought it best to offer something brief in reply.

"Wow! A pair of heavy cases there, Bobby. I'm at a loss for words. I hope the best for you in that regard."

Mickey then moved on to the next subject.

"So, how's the back door business been going for y'all?"

"Things been going fairly well, I suppose. I've been busy through the years. Moving the family from the back door area of things to the front. My plan is to legalize us in all areas," Bobby said.

"The booze too?" Mickey asked.

He turned his head to the left to have a look at Bobby as they continued to walk slowly.

"Yep. That too. We've got a distillery now in our namesake—after my father actually—Paul Kavanaugh. The bottles of bourbon we now produce have the potential to give Jack Daniels a run for its customer base. A business is only good as its competitor, Mickey. You know?"

"That's a good thing there, Bobby, a real good thing. But on the flip side, I wanted to meet with you here to discuss something about Miss Peaches. And another thing," Mickey stated. He was now eager to get down to the meat and potatoes of the conversation.

"And what might that one other thing be?"

Bobby's interest was now perked. Mickey paused. He then took a look at Bobby once more, trying to determine in his mind whether or not to speak to him about what he so badly wanted to talk with him about. Reluctantly, he let it out. A piece of it, so to speak.

"How about if I told you I knew a thing or two concerning one of those troubling cases of yours?"

Bobby froze then and there in his tracks and took a look at Mickey. He had a hard expression about his face.

"Mickey, please don't tell me you had something to do with that poor little Maddox gal being taken advantage of and killed, did you?" he asked. "Lord knows don't tell me that. I don't know how I'd take it."

"Nooo, Bobby! Not that one. And I didn't say I had something to do with anything. I mentioned I might *know* a thing or two concerning."

Mickey knew it was important to be clear with Bobby on exactly what he'd said.

"My apologies to you there. That was what you said. But what is it you were referring to?"

"The disappearance of those two policemen," Mickey said.

He managed to stun Bobby with those words, causing them to stop walking once more. Bobby took another stern look at Mickey.

"What!" Bobby blurted. "How much you know of this?"

"Quite a deal, possibly."

"And why you just now bringing this to my attention?"

"Because I didn't know how to tell you. I was afraid. Thought you may have *me* locked up. That was one of the main reasons why I left the way that I did. And why Miss Peaches had done the same."

"Really!" "Yes sir, Bobby."

"Well, please let me know what you know. Since you done broke the ice and revealed this much," he urged.

"Turns out, Bobby, these two missing cops aren't actually missing after all, my friend."

"Continue on. I'm listening."

"Well, I have it on good authority, that those two boys—the policemen Flaherty and Carson—fled the country to escape potential prosecution for the crimes that they'd committed."

"What crimes?"

"The kidnapping, rape, and murder of that poor little innocent Maddox girl! That crime, Bobby. And those associated with it," Mickey stated. He dramatized the way he worded his lie to Bobby.

"Huh!" the prosecutor let out. He was appalled at the revelations.

Bobby now looked at Mickey with a serious eye.

"What more can you tell me?"

"Well, the two cops got out of the country and headed in different directions. Flaherty made his way to Ireland from what I heard through the grapevine over the years. And Carson, he went to Mexico to catch a little fresh air. My sources I've kept on payroll keep me informed. You already know we had a lot of police boys pass through our pleasure houses. And with her—one of my sources—knowing as much as she does about things, it became too much for her to bear any longer," Mickey related.

"So, what you're telling me is that the disappearance of those policemen, is directly connected to the Maddox girl's murder? That's what you're saying to me?"

"That's exactly what I'm saying, Bobby. The real story to those two. Whether you knew it or not, the Maddox girl worked under Miss Peaches at the house she operated. Flaherty and Carson would come by there many days to see her. One late night, the police boys forced their way into her house, snatched up the poor girl, and took her away with them. To where, we don't know. Word circulating with the other girls was that the older one—Flaherty—had an accident he'd committed with her, and needed to do something at all costs, to keep that secret of his from getting out. That's what I know, Bobby."

Mickey managed to piece together a well-spoken lie. It was so beautiful that Bobby had no choice but to believe it, whether he wanted to or not. Also, at the time when Flaherty and Carson was alive, a scandal of some sort was going on inside the police department that involved Flaherty. Bobby knew of this prior to being elected District Attorney. Mickey himself knew of the scandal, but had no knowledge of who it was concerning.

"And Evelyn can confirm all your now telling me, you say?" asked Bobby.

"Miss Peaches is gonna confirm all I'm now saying to you, once the two of you get back to the hotel suite," Mickey responded confidently.

"Well, I be damned! Two of my top cases are directly related. I wouldn't have ever thought that to be. But from the sound of the music you just sang into my ear, there's reason to believe this may be true. I can't quite understand the whole issue about a caller anonymously reporting a blue Cadillac taking a journey down to the riverbank at that hour of the night with a black male driving and a white female on the passenger side. And then, only the male leaving alone. If someone could just make some sense of that for me. Then I'll see the bigger picture," Bobby stated.

Mickey had a thought. It was related to something Bobby had said.

"You mentioned, Lieutenant Wilkens, was the one who got the call from the one reporting, right?"

"Right."

"And about a month or two before this 'so called' anonymous person making a report, this same lieutenant—

Pecan Slim—so happened to pull me and my people over in a blue Cadillac that I owned, because he thought it was stolen, right? Until I had him contact you to relieve me of the harassment of his traffic stop, right?"

"Make your point for me, Mickey. Too much elaboration blurs the picture," Bobby said, urging him to speak straight.

"In my view, it's a cover up, Bobby. Wilkens and Flaherty needed a scapegoat as a smokescreen to cover the scandal brewing about cops pulling over women, then sexually assaulting them. Not to mention the fact about cops raiding *cathouses* and extorting women out of sexual favors so as not to be arrested and booked on prostitution charges," Mickey stated. "All the pieces to the puzzle are there. I simply had to put it together before I had the opportunity to meet with you."

Bobby accepted the whole scenario Mickey laid out to him.

"You make a strong point, Mickey. Now that I think about it, that damn Pecan Slim and Dickey Flaherty were always fond of one another. And had that been the body of a little black girl found raped and murdered, Dickie probably would have been the one reporting a call from an anonymous person to cover for Pecan Slim. Due to how head over heels Pecan Slim can get over a black cunt. But it was a white female, Flaherty's preference. So that gives credibility to your story. They're covering for one another, potentially. And now, I've got to get Internal Affairs to dig to see what we can turn up, if anything, due to how long it's been. But we'll see," Bobby stated.

The two men continued to walk more and talk along the lines of other topics. There was a lot more to unpack.

Chapter 26

Prior to the meeting with Bobby, Mickey was sure to thoroughly go over everything with Miss Peaches on what they were to perpetrate to Bobby. He knew long ago that it was important to come up with a story and a solid plan to save his ass from the potential prosecution of the truth of his past actions were to come to the light. His worry through the years had caused him more trouble than he could bargain for, leading up to the day he spoke with Bobby.

Mickey had one last scheme in mind to put to use and to keep dominant power, because Bobby now had him under his thumbscrew. For this particular play, he would need Miss Peaches to agree with him. Mickey knew that Bobby would want to sex her at every available opportunity he had while still down in Miami. He was able to convince her to allow Bobby to release himself inside her. The plan was to have him unknowingly impregnate Miss Peaches. This occurred on three different occasions while they were together at the Tropicana Hotel and Resort in South Beach Miami, Florida.

Mickey needed leverage over Bobby, for security purposes, in the event that the original story he gave bottomed out and fell apart. It wasn't likely that it would. He had to be sure. And Miss Peaches, having a baby by a married DA, through an affair that had been carried on for many years, would be more than enough blackmail material to hang over Bobby's head for years to come. Bobby had better continue to act right if he knew what was best for him, and if he wanted to continue to be re-elected to hold the office he now held.

Everyone enjoyed the fight there in Miami and the much-needed vacation. The camaraderie and joy they experienced in being able to see and talk with one another together again was an occasion to be remembered. And so, Mickey's plan was in progress. The plot thickened. Miss Peaches related the whole story as Mickey needed her to, and in the exact way he wanted her to put it. Although Bobby still held skepticism in his own way, he felt compelled to believe them until it proved otherwise that he couldn't.

Back in Philly . . .

Josephine had begun to develop a not so pleasant view of her husband. Her heart and thoughts had taken a turn from what they originally were, and she was now falling out of love with Mickey faster than she'd fallen into it. The life thought to come with him had not become a reality. She now resented the thought. All she had the time to do was to keep home and look after all those damn kids they had. JoJo was technically a little young lady living in a shoe, and had so many children she didn't know what to do.

On this particular day, Natalie was at her house from New Jersey to visit. JoJo wanted to have a conversation with her about how the marriage with Mickey was going. She brought up the acquaintance between him and Miss Peaches, a topic Mickey specifically told her never to mention to no one else, not even family.

"Natalie, truth be told, I really don't know how much longer I can take this. This isn't the life I envisioned for myself at twenty-three," JoJo said. Her tone of voice was somber and distressing.

"What you mean, you don't know how much longer you can take this, JoJo? You don't have much of a choice. That what you signed up for, remember?"

"And even that wasn't right, Natalie. Mickey paid somebody to make the paperwork say I was older than I really was. He's a manipulator." JoJo revealed her true feeling of the man she said I do to.

"Well, five kids later, a big ol' pretty house to live in, and now living in a larger city in the north out the country of the south, that don't sound like the moves of a manipulator would make. It must be something else that ails you, JoJo."

JoJo got quiet for a moment. She had a look of shame about her face.

"It is, Natalie," she confirmed.

She continued to sit on the edge of the bed with her head hung low and her emotions getting the best of her. It was a Sunday afternoon. Her kids were all in their rooms playing with toys, and Mickey, he was still away down South handling business. Natalie took a seat on the bed next to her sibling, put her arm around her, and did all she could to encourage JoJo to let her know what was the matter. She saw that JoJo was deeply bothered about something.

"What's the problem, JoJo? Talk to me, please."

JoJo looked into Natalie's eyes. A tear streamed down her own face as she prepared to relate the trouble that was going on in paradise.

"Mickey hasn't turned out to be half the man I originally thought he would. He's never home to help me take care of all these babies he's put in me. He don't listen to anything that I say to him as I try to explain I'm falling apart. All he does is dictate to me how to do things the way he wants them done, not how I best know to do them. And Mickey is a drug dealer and in the streets too deep. We've got kids, Natalie. That type of lifestyle is totally unacceptable," JoJo expressed. Her eyes went back to the floor. "He's got another woman too, Natalie," she now reluctantly revealed.

The dark side to Mickey was brought to the light by his wife. His naked soul was exposed.

"What! JoJo! That can't be!"

"Yep. And he had the nerve to bring her here. To our house."

"You gotta be lying to me!"

More tears now streamed down her face.

"I'm telling you the truth, Nat. Some woman named 'Miss Peaches.' She claim to have been doing the nasty with other men for Mickey since she was sixteen."

"Huh!" "Yep."

"So, she's from down South too, right?"

"She said she was. I'm just pissed off at the fact he didn't make me aware of her sooner. The way he did it was all messed up. He didn't put me on notice or didn't check with me to see how I may feel about things before he took it upon himself to bring a hooker to our house," JoJo lamented.

"JoJo! You mean to tell me, Mickey had the nerve to bring some random woman to y'all house without you knowing, and expected for everything to just be all strawberries and cream? Or in this case, 'Peaches' and cream?" Natalie was appalled at the notion.

"Yep." She then pursed her lips and began to cry harder.

"That's exactly what he's done. And then he goes on to tell me, 'There are gonna be some days Peaches will be staying with our family here in our house, and other days she'll be at the hotel.' What kind of moonshine he thought I was on to go for something like that? He may have gotten me drunk the night we met, but that's a time long gone."

"The only thing I can think of with a situation like this is those two must got something heavy on one another for him to want to keep her close like that. I'm almost sure she'll be living here in Philadelphia before long."

"That may be true. And if she's got something heavy on him to hang over his head to make him acknowledge her, then guess what! So do I," JoJo expressed in a vehement way. She appeared to be vindictive now. Salty about it all.

"And what's that?"

In a reluctant but burdensome relieving way, JoJo began to spill the beans to Natalie and relate the exact truth about all she knew regarding the shooting deaths of those two policemen—Flaherty and Carson. The reality of the potential consequences JoJo could face if the truth had ever gotten out. The fear became too much to bear. JoJo was terrified and now, so was Natalie. She knew nothing about anything. All she remembered was her husband Johnny Mack bringing JoJo to their house in the middle of the night and telling her to pack as fast as she could, that they had to leave town. JoJo's confirming things now had Natalie just as fearful as her sister, if not more.

***

Not long before the day, JoJo had gotten a job for an elder white lady, Mrs. Thelma Hammock, who was in the home décor business. JoJo loved to buy material from her shop in downtown Philly, so as to fix up the home she and Mickey owned. An acquaintance was established between the two ladies.

The job JoJo now had now required that they travel locally throughout the state and region, and other states to fulfill contracts. Her younger sister Sasha now lived in the north with them so she could continue her help with the kids. Sasha graduated high school and now needed a form of income. JoJo paid her well. And not only that, if JoJo ever felt the urgency to take the kids and up and leave Mickey, Miss Hammock had family in New Hampshire and could expand the business there and have JoJo run it. Sasha would have the kids throughout the day as JoJo worked. The bottom line was she had options.

Natalie—now knowing the truth—absolutely encouraged JoJo to get the hell away from Mickey at all costs. She feared for her and JoJo at an all-time high. Two highly decorated white cops being slaughtered and concealed had a severe penalty behind it. And now the question remained in Natalie's mind, what happened to the bodies of those cops? What did Johnny Mack and Mickey do to them? She'd never know.

Chapter 27

For Bobby Kavanaugh, it didn't take long for him to get busy in his hunt for the truth behind the issue with those missing cops. He felt the need to know whether or not they were dead or alive. All that was known was they were missing and had been so for six years on-going. For the most part, he accepted the story Mickey related. It seemed authentic because it fit the character of the two policemen. However, Bobby needed something to corroborate those accounts Mickey made. And to achieve his objective to know the truth, Bobby contacted the FBI to involve them.

A nationwide and international manhunt was put in place at the time. Also, bulletin-board-sized photos of Flaherty and Carson were put up in all the southern states, and especially those bordered with Mexico. Bobby was also sure to have the FBI contact Ireland's authorities as well, so as to leave no avenue unexplored. In addition, Bobby had a follow-up conversation with now Captain Jimmy Wilkens. He'd been promoted from lieutenant. Wilkens reiterated his position and pointed the finger at Mickey Savage. Bobby and

Wilkens had a conversation regarding the matter. This was after Bobby had met with Mickey.

"So, Captain Wilkens, just so we're clear on this," Bobby initiated. "Your theory is that those two policemen of ours—Lieutenant Flaherty and Sergeant Carson—had made it their business as part of the investigation into the rape and murder of the female whose body was discovered back in fifty-eight down by the river, to arrest and question a potential suspect— 'Methuselah Savage' aka Mickey Savage? And upon them doing so, the suspect became opposed to the actions of the policemen, then attacked them, killing both and leaving no bodies to be found by authorities?" "That's exactly what I strongly believe took place. And knowing what I know, I'm sticking to that theory. I'm the one who provided those officers with the sound information that I'd been provided. And at the time, I was notified by Lieutenant Flaherty directly that he and his partner would apprehend Savage to question him. Neither myself nor the station heard from those two officers anymore from that day. And we hadn't seen Methuselah Savage or his Cadillac either. So, you tell me, what do you think took place?" Wilkens responded. "Not to mention the fact that the car the suspect owned wasn't a stolen vehicle."

"I understand the position you've taken, Captain Wilkens. You're on the side of the law enforcement. So am I. But I'm eager to know how does your theory coincide with what actually took place? Facts we don't know for certain."

"District Attorney Kavanaugh, I'm telling you. There's not a doubt in my mind. Methuselah Savage had everything to do with the disappearance of my fellow men of law. And also, the rape and murder of the innocent female. You find that lowly bastard Savage, and therein lies the answer to both cases. Now I'm totally aware that there's been several other high-profile cases that occurred through the years that warrant your attention. But I still have my view that Savage is guilty. And I'm confident someone will come forward with information to help us put the remaining pieces to the mystery together. A family member of his or somebody. Now we have the federal government to assist us, the process should be less difficult."

Bobby and Wilkens continued to trade bars on relevant points pertaining to cases. They'd even pulled the file of the Norma Maddox case. Bobby took notice of the report from the medical examiner revealing a gold hoop earring of the victim was missing. Only one was found still in place on the earlobe. The body also had two broken-off fingernails from the right hand. The index and middle fingers specifically. The case was still very complex.

***

Kit Lansing, the male photographer who had been hired by Seth Kavanaugh to do photoshoots at the modeling agency once owned by Seth had relocated from Georgia to San Diego, California. His reason for up and skipping town was due to the disturbing news of the body of Norma Maddox having been found. This was the last client he'd worked with prior to her murder. He had firsthand knowledge of the last people the victim was with and came to no other conclusion outside of Seth and Jeremy being the perpetrators of that crime. Judging by how obsessed Seth demonstrated he was over the young lady and to prevent from being harmed himself behind all he possessed and knew, Kit got out of the way. Far away.

Through the years, Kit followed the story. Not once did he take notice of Seth appearing on the news or in the newspaper to express his condolences, his sorrow, or any form of sympathy towards someone he hired to work for him, and whom he deemed as a friend. Seth didn't so much make a statement to the police or show a stance with the girl's family in the aftermath of her death. And for Kit, that didn't sit too well with him, knowing what he knew. Not to mention how crazed and caring Seth showed to be over Lady Maddox. It was all a fake.

While doing a photo shoot one day along the beach in San Diego, Kit took notice of the striking resemblance the client he now worked with had to Lady Maddox. Their figures and poses were similar. He made mention of this to her. She asked, "Do you have any surviving photos of her?" He had.

Kit showed them, then went on to tell the story of their brief acquaintance and her horrific demise. The young lady was brought to tears behind his revelation. Kit went on to tell her what he suspected, and about Seth and Jeremy. The client strongly encouraged him to contact the FBI and Savannah authorities. To also provide copies of the photos of Lady Maddox he had, especially those that had Seth up close and personal with her in them. Seth had paid extra money for this and demanded his inclusion. Kit did as Seth instructed. This might be the thing to help crack the case and prevent an innocent man, Mickey Savage, from having to take the fall once the truth comes to the light.

Kit then put together two separate packages containing the photos he had. Most notably, those that had Lady Maddox and Seth together in them, and a few that had her posing alongside Seth's brown Cadillac, a car he still owned. He mailed one to the FBI in Georgia and one to the District Attorney's office in Savannah. Both had anonymous sender written on them, and accompanied with a note. Kit spilled his guts on all he knew and made a special request that justice be served for Norma Elaine Maddox. He prayed for her as well.

***

Dating back to the day Seth maliciously took advantage of Lady Maddox sexually then killed her in the process, he'd begun his search high and low for the photographer he'd hired to do the photo shoot, Kit Lansing. Seth knew Kit possessed both, knowledge of him being last seen with the young model, and photos of them together to condemn him once shit hit the fan. And at all costs, he felt he had to find Kit and have him eliminated, long before Kit could run to the police and expose what he knew. Even with the hired killers to assist him in his hunt, Seth had no luck locating Kit. It was as if he'd fallen from the face of earth.

The six years of not knowing where Kit had disappeared to, caused Seth a great deal of mental torment and severe bouts of anxiety. He wanted Kit dead! And he wouldn't be able to rest on no accord until he knew he was put away. Forever. Seth's plot to have Mickey take the fall had failed. And no other arrests were made to free him from blame. Not only that, Seth also didn't know whether or not his friend Jeremy would fold under police pressure if they ever arrested and questioned him. Something had to be done, so thought Seth.

He knew that the crime of murder was the only one that did not have a statute of limitation. And the great state of Georgia, didn't discriminate when it came to the guilty person of such high offense. The Peach State would send a white killer to the electric chair at the same speed they would a black killer. It made no difference if convicted in a court of law.

Chapter 28

Three Months Later . . .

The marriage between JoJo and Mickey became more complicated and estranged by the day. She absolutely hated the relationship he had going on with Miss Peaches, but knew there was nothing that could be done about it. To JoJo, it appeared that Mickey's mind and heart belonged to Miss Peaches, while his kids belonged to her. Nothing more. Not even the love they once shared. JoJo was fed up with the many days and nights Mickey was away from home, out and about in the streets, and not putting forth any effort to help raise his kids. Her pleas to him to do better by his family seemed to fall on deaf ears, and he paid her no mind when she let him know she was on the verge of losing it mentally.

A nervous breakdown was near to her. Being left with no other option, she felt, JoJo packed bags for her and the five kids and prepared to leave. She took a hundred and fifty thousand of the three hundred thousand Mickey had stashed there at their home, got in the car and left Philly, headed to New Hampshire to live. Mrs. Hammock recommended this.

JoJo long proved to be trustworthy and a fine worker for the elder white lady and was afforded the opportunity to establish a business there in the New England state for Mrs. Hammock. She simply had to get away from the no-good husband she had, along with the evil activity he was involved in.

The day after she'd left, Mickey finally made it home from a long night out and about the town. He had a large amount of cash with him and JoJo was supposed to count it up once he got there. It was money he intended to put away towards the kids' education once they'd come of age. Man he was in for a huge surprise. He entered and immediately took notice that the house was quieter than it normally would be on a Saturday morning. All the TVs were off and not a sound came through the house. Before he could call out for JoJo, he spotted a letter on the living room table she'd left for him. Mickey slowly walked over to retrieve it. He took a hard look at it then began to read. He couldn't believe the choice of words JoJo used. They were stern and deliberate. The main portion stood out. She brought up the fact about how she felt exactly behind shooting those two cops and causing their deaths. JoJo mentioned how much she feared for her and the kids. She excluded him. In addition, she threw it in his face of how terrible of a husband and father he was and how much she resented him now.

Miss Peaches tend to be more the wife of yours and have your heart than I do! I despise you, Mickey! If only you knew.

The letter concluded. Mickey sat the note back on the table, walked over to his whisky cellar, took out a bottle of his best bourbon, opened the top cabinet to the cellar, picked out a cigar to smoke, then made his way to the leather recliner. He took a seat, poured up a drink, lit his cigar, then lay back in the chair to relax. He really needed to clear his conscience and gain a piece of mind.

Mickey drank then puffed—drank and puffed and repeated several times. He cussed like a sailor at no one in particular. After a few shots of alcohol and several tokes from the expensive Cuban cigar, Mickey stood to his feet, staggered momentarily, then went over to the record player and put on an album by the legendary Miles Davis, *Seven Steps: The Complete Columbia Recordings of 1963-1964*. He took his seat once more, struck a match to light his cigar again—French-inhaling twice over—then slowly releasing the thick smoke from his system. Dude was at a loss for words. He was also unsure what course of action he could take. It crossed his mind that maybe JoJo would return once she was no longer mad. But for him to know where she'd gone off to and confirm when she might come back, Mickey called Johnny Mack's home.

"Savage residence," Natalie answered.

She was just the person he wanted to speak with directly.

"Natalie," he uttered her name. "I'm sure you know why I'm calling. I wanna speak with you. Not Johnny Mack."

"Mickey, I'mma just tell you straight up, okay? I ain't got nothing to do with y'all business. I'm not gonna get in the middle of it." "Well, can you at least tell me where she ran off to with my kids?" he pleaded.

"I can't do that either, Mickey. That'll be putting me and Johnny Mack in the middle of it. But what I can tell you is that you took it too far with what you got going on with that Miss Peaches *thang* you involved with. That was what really did it."

"Judging by the way that sounded, I'm assuming JoJo came to you for advice and let you know how she was feeling?"

"Look, Mickey. I'm aware my sister was young and dumb and hadn't had any sex at the time you met her. But now she's older and wiser, and got five kids by you she's gotta take care of. So of course, she came to me—her big sister—to talk about y'all issues and asked what to do about them."

"So, it was you who told her to leave me high and dry?"

"I sure did. I told JoJo to follow her heart and do what was best for her and those kids. And she didn't leave you 'high and dry'!" Natalie retorted. You got Miss Peaches, don't you! She can help you pull through. And not only that. JoJo terrified behind that little incident of yours down in Georgia when we all had to up and leave in the middle of the night from our home for good, behind something you got going on. That added to the reason why she wanted to put distance between you two. Not to mention the illegal activities you got operating in those streets. My sister's reasons are endless, Mickey," she stated emphatically.

Mickey looked shocked at how Natalie was talking to him. He couldn't believe what he was hearing. He defended his character.

"Just so you're reminded, Natalie. Those illegal activities you brought up… they're the same ones that paid for the house you live in, for the car you drive, and for the food that my business partner—your husband—put on your table from the money produced. So don't try to give me that B.S. sermon on the mount speech about who's right and who's not!" Mickey spat.

"I'm hanging up this phone now before we go too far and say something we both regret."

"Yeah! I bet you are, ain't you!" he vented in retort before Natalie banged the phone back on the hook.

He sat motionlessly in the chair. His face was construed to an angry demeanor, and the wheels in his head began to turn like crazy now. He didn't know what JoJo might fuck up and say to someone about what really happened to those two cops. He had no idea either what she'd do. Those fears of hers were expressed to him one too many times, and he knew it was important at that point to put them to rest. Eternally.

Truth be, the evil thought did pass through Mickey's mind that the best way to rid himself of the threat was to simply whack JoJo, his young tender wife, and that'd be the end of it all. It was an act he could consider, over awaiting her to run to the police and report what he'd done six summers in their past. Those high-powered racist crackers in Georgia wouldn't hesitate to fry Mickey's black ass if his truth came out, and he knew this. The problem was that his stupid ass wife didn't, and she looked to not care. Mickey wanted to keep all his options open to him so in case of emergency, to break glass. Nothing was left off the table with a resolution. What would have to be done couldn't wait.

Chapter 29

Down In Georgia . . .

Bobby Kavanaugh had received a private call from an essential work professional he had an acquaintance with. It was a doctor by the name of Henry Turner. He had something of importance to relate to him. Back in 1958, Doctor Turner had performed a medical procedure, and treatment had taken place but the facts of Seth's visit to him were still relevant. And the doctor simply wanted to be of help in some type of way.

The case of Norma Elaine Maddox was back in the news. It hadn't really gone away. Only pushed to the cold case files until someone came forward with information to heat things up again. Someone had. An anonymous sender of photos and a note. The FBI was now in on the case. And there was only so much that Bobby could do now to keep the truth of something his nephew had an involvement with from being exposed, judging from the compilation of photos he'd received himself in the mail. In addition, the FBI contacted him as well and demanded that he look farther into the matter. Bobby monitored Seth but didn't mention anything to him.

"Bobby Kavanaugh here," he answered.

"Bobby. Hey. How you doing? It's me. Henry Turner. You got a minute?" the doctor asked.

"Hey, Doc. I'm good, buddy. Sure, I've got a minute. What you got?"

"I'm afraid you may not want to hear this."

"Uh-oh! This can't be good. But go on. I'm listening."

"I've noticed one of your more serious cases has resurfaced in the news again. The one about the Maddox girl."

"Yeah. That case. It has been back in the media of late. The investigation opened again. We're getting closer to cracking it. Hopefully soon. You got any information that may help?"

"Actually, I do. The circumstances of the case, and the evidence I've come to learn of are just too coincidental for me to overlook, Bobby. This is more than a nullity here, I believe."

"Sounds to me, Doctor, like you have something of importance to relate to me. What is it?"

"Well, to be straight to the point with you, back around the time when this particular case first occurred, a nephew of yours came to me to be treated for a terrible bacterial infection that had set inside his body in two separate locations. He had a bite wound to the chest, and two nail puncture wounds to the left area of his torso. Two orange painted nails were removed. They were the main cause of infection to that part of the body," stated Doctor Turner.

The missing orange painted nails immediately stood out in Bobby's mind. He now had the photos of the victim to corroborate that the nails could possibly belong to Lady Maddox, the girl who his nephew was in the photos with. All was left at that point was for Doctor Turner to confirm which particular nephew of his he'd treated, and that would be enough for Bobby to begin an investigation into the past bad actions of a family member of his. He had an oath of office to uphold as DA, and the law dictated that he does.

"You got to be frigging kidding me, Doc. Which nephew of mine you treated?"

"It was Seth. And not only that, I still have those nails that were dug from his body. Along with photos I took of his wounds. The law here in Georgia—as you know—allows medical professionals to hold onto medical records of a patient for up to seven years."

"I'm aware, Doctor Turner. I'd like a copy of Seth's medical file and what you treated him for. Those photos as well. How soon could you get it to me?"

"I'm afraid I can't do that blatantly, Bobby. That'll violate patient-doctor confidentiality I'm obligated to oblige by. I could lose my license."

"Not if I have a warrant signed by a judge to authorize the inspection of those documents. They may be pertinent to an investigation."

"Now, that's a different story altogether. You know how to locate me. What do you plan to do, have one of your assistants come over the office to retrieve them?"

"No, Doc. I'll personally appear to pick them up. And if you will, I respectfully ask that you keep this as quiet as could be, Doctor Turner. Don't even mention anything to Seth, okay?"

"Gotcha, buddy."

"But let me ask you something, Doctor Turner."

"What's that, Bobby?"

"What interest do you have with this case? What prompted you to contact me to relate all you have?"

"Because, Bobby, I'm in the interest of justice. I advocate law and order. That Maddox girl could've been my daughter. And when I took notice of the case in the news again, and the mention of the victim fighting off her attacker, possibly clawing and biting, my mind immediately went back to the day I treated Seth. The bite wound to his chest and the infections he suffered, were consistent to the reports made by authorities. I know you, and knew it was important to call and bring this to your attention," Doctor Turner stated. "And lastly on that, not once since the day I treated Seth had he asked about his medical file, not until after the day the case showed back up in the news. This added to my concern. I had to contact you."

"Well, I thank you, Doctor Turner. And I'll be by your office with the proper authorization to have those medical documents, those nails you still have, and those photos. Okay?"

"Not a problem, Bobby. I'm here. And you'll be by when exactly?"

"Today. If I'm successful in having Judge Clements sign off on the warrant I seek."

"That's good to know. Nice speaking with you again. Take care," Doctor Turner lastly said.

"You as well."

The call concluded.

Bobby was left in an ugly predicament. He now had to possibly initiate an investigation on a family member of his for the rape and murder of a young female. And if that were to be so, there would be no way the Kavanaugh name could remain in good grace with the law-abiding public in the county. The citizens would never forgive them if a conviction came about. Bobby was now eager to get down to the bottom of what his nephew had concealed for years.

***

Bobby pulled the Norma Maddox case files from the shelf to go over yet again. He discovered stark confirmation. The autopsy report indicated indeed that two fingernails from the right hand had broken off and were missing.

Doctor Turner did state something to the effect of removing two orange painted nails from Seth's body, Bobby thought.

The autopsy report mentioned the victim had bloodstained teeth on the upper row. Bobby read over that portion once more. He also said Seth had a bite wound to the chest as well, he farther thought. Reluctantly, Bobby had no choice but to go to the chamber of Superior Court Judge Howard G. Clements, to secure a warrant to inspect the medical flies and if necessary, the home and the vehicle of his nephew. The time was 11:30 A.M. Still early. Bobby had ample opportunity to have his warrant signed and be able to make it to Doctor Turner's office before the sun was set. He took to the mission at hand.

Chapter 30

Bobby was granted the authority to move forward with the legal process he had going on. He made his way to Doctor Turner. He'd been provided the written medical documents, the nails, and an articulated explanation of the medical terminology that related to the type of infections caused by the saliva-laden wound and the fungal wounds from the nails. Bobby was handed the photos of Seth's wounds as well. His nephew had serious explaining to do.

Bobby stayed at his office late that day and mulled over possible theories with the material at his disposal. A crucial point of interest stood out to him. A person who might hold the key to it all. Someone Bobby knew his nephew kept with him as a friend, a driver, and as an assistant—Jeremy. Bobby needed to get to him, to know what he had to say, if anything. But Bobby had no warrant for him and couldn't simply violate Jeremy's rights in an attempt to gain more information which might help to solve the case. However, there was no law to prevent law authorities from coercing

Jeremy to come of his own to the DA's office to talk about other things that may lead to a series of questions along the lines of the Maddox case Bibby had to now figure out how to get Jeremy without him alerting Seth and informing him that he was under investigation. Bobby had a plan.

One Day Later . . .

Jeremy Crowder was contacted by the DA's office regarding, "His proper practice of his right to bear arms, and to carry concealed weapons. They wanted to ensure that gun owners continued good habits and follow the law." Bobby had his secretary to perpetrate a well-told lie to Jeremy. He was there to have a conversation. Bobby's assistant put a few questions to Jeremy along the lines of what he'd been consulted about over the phone. Then walked in Bobby, the DA himself. Someone Jeremy knew all too well.

"Hey there, Jeremy! How you been?" Bobby said to him. He had a warm smile about his face to keep Jeremy calm, so as to not force him to invoke his right to remain silent and walk out.

"Hey, Mister Bobby. DA Kavanaugh, I meant. My apologies," Jeremy responded.

"That's okay. Call me Bobby. That's the name you know me by. You keeping those guns of yours properly put away?"

"Of course, I am, Mister Bobby. Hopefully, that's all this meeting is about?"

"It is. That's unless you've got something else to share with me. Why else would you make such remark in that way?"

Bobby was provided an angle to penetrate.

"I don't know if you're aware or not. But here in Georgia, it's a crime to have knowledge of a crime that has been committed, or to witness one being done, and not do anything to stop it, or report it. That'll make someone a 'Party to a Crime.' And anyone convicted of that gets the same amount of time as the person who actually committed it. The 'death penalty' included, Jeremy. Unless that party to a crime 'fesses up. The first to do so and then we go light on them. You understand my point to you, son?" he drilled.

He spoke slowly and deliberately. Although Bobby merely recited a particular code of law in Georgia, Jeremy began to get paranoid at that point. He trembled, broke into a sweat, and showed signs of anxiety coming on.

"Mister Bobby . . . I . . . ah . . . ah . . . ain't done nothing wrong, sir," Jeremy uttered broken words.

"So, you trying to tell me someone else did something wrong you know about? And you don't want to say? That's being a party to a crime, Jeremy. And you know my family well enough to know, we're law following people, don't you? Now, you and my nephew Seth have been buddies since you two were young. I'm only hoping you and him don't know anything about a crime that's been committed and haven't brought it to my attention."

Bobby slyly put together a scenario to place on Jeremy's mind.

"There's something terribly wrong with you, Jeremy. I can tell. What's eating at your conscience, son? Talk to me."

Anxiety gained the best of Jeremy. He tilted forward onto the table from his seat in the interview room. Suddenly, he threw up the meal he'd eaten not long before the visit there. The carpet was now a mess. A foul odor made the situation more unpleasant. Bobby didn't let up. He drilled harder.

"I'm about to have the police arrest you, Jeremy. Because I believe you know something you're refusing to come forward about," Bobby threatened. "And if it's one thing I hate most, Jeremy, is a heinous crime on my desk that I can't solve. Like the one of that pretty little innocent model girl, Norma Maddox. About six years ago, she was raped and murdered by some sick monster! Or a sicko with someone else. And I won't rest until I nail their asses!"

Chapter 31

Bobby took a stern look into Jeremy's eyes. He caused him to tense up at the mention of Lady Maddox. Jeremy eyes bulged. Bobby knew he could break him at that point.

"I'mma ask you one time only, Jeremy. Because I believe you could help, Okay? Now, who killed—"

"Seth did it, Mister Bobby! He was the one raped that girl and choked her to death, then tried to put it on the nigger guy he sold the blue Cadillac to!" Jeremy blurted in confession. "I saw him do it!"

Bobby continued to look at Jeremy and smiled. His ploy had worked.

"I was going to ask you who killed Abraham Lincoln! But since you mentioned that... I ain't got no choice now but to question you about that. What else you got to tell me? Speak up, Jeremy!"

He confessed his part.

"I'm glad you spoke the truth. Hopefully, it'll set you free, Jeremy."

Bobby then pulled a photo of Norma Maddox and showed it to Jeremy.

"Is this the girl here you talking about? Is she the one Seth raped and choked to death?"

Jeremy nodded his head to indicate yes.

"Speak up for me please, Jeremy. I need you to say it," Bobby instructed.

"Yes, Mister Bobby. That's the girl. The Maddox girl," Jeremy replied.

"I originally thought she was a girlfriend of his or female companion."

"They didn't have any relationship in that sense. She was a model for the agency Seth owned. He became obsessed with her, Mister Bobby."

Bobby thumbed through the photos once more. Were you all in Seth's brown Cadillac when all this took place?"

"Yes, sir."

"And you were the driver while they rode in the backseat?"

"I was."

"Where were y'all coming from? Where were y'all headed?" Bobby pressed.

It was now a full-scale interrogation.

"We were leaving a photo shoot on the beach in Tybee Island, and was supposed to have taken Lady Maddox to the hotel where she stayed. That never happened."

"You mentioned her by her modeling name. You knew her?"

"Not really. I'd only met her the few times I had to drive for Seth to the photoshoots."

"Okay. Let's back up a moment. You said, 'That never happened.' What never happened?" Bobby asked.

"Us making it to the hotel to drop her off."

"Well, why not?"

"Seth couldn't control himself. He'd gotten excited about her. He couldn't handle being turned down by her for sex."

"He couldn't?"

"No sir, Mister Bobby."

"So, what exactly did he do?"

"He took her against her will," Jeremy let out.

"He took her against her will as in raped her, you mean. Is that what you mean?"

"Mister Bobby, that's your nephew we're talking about here. My best friend." Jeremy pleaded for mercy with his choice of words.

"Justice, Jeremy… is always on the side of the righteous, son. It doesn't matter who you are. Right is right, while wrong is wrong. And that's all there is to it."

"Mister Bobby, I never thought Seth would turn out to be that type of person. He wouldn't stop. He'd turned into a monster of some sort."

"One who would hold a woman down against her will, with his hands locked tight around her throat, while forcefully thrusting his poisonous spear into her womanhood as she bit and clawed with all she had, trying to free herself from underneath that monster and his weight," Bobby vented in disgust his theory of the bad acts his brother's son had committed.

In addition to Jeremy revealing the horrific details of the crime he and Seth carried out, he spoke about what he knew about the contraband pick-up and drop-off spot near the river the Kavanaugh clan used. That same location dated back to the days of Prohibition. The family's riches and wealth were generated along the current of the Savannah River. The Kavanaugh's now had a profitable sugar mill and bourbon distillery from the illicit dollars they'd made in the Roaring Twenties and Dirty Thirties. Bobby knew then and there that Jeremy knew far too much of the family's underworld activities and could bring them down. He had to do something to silence him regarding such. Bobby waved for his two assistants to enter the room. He now wanted Jeremy taken into custody.

"Cuff him and call the police to come pick him up. He's being charge as a party to a crime for the rape and murder of Norma Elaine Maddox," Bobby ordered.

Jeremy had a down-trodden look on his face. He then began to cry. The two assistants told him to stand, and they took to placing the cuffs on his wrists.

"What about your nephew, Seth, Mister Bobby? He's the one who committed the crime. Are you gonna have him arrested too?" blurted Jeremy.

He took the prosecutor by surprise with the utterance of those words in the presence of the others. Bobby gave him a scathing look. He was made angrier by his outburst. Jeremy caused the others to have a concerned look at their boss. They didn't know how much truth there was to what the now arrested man stated. Nonetheless, it was out there, and there was nothing Bobby could do to force it from the minds of all who heard it.

Jeremy repeated himself as he was being escorted to a holding cell. He felt it was important to get that out, in order to not take the fall by himself.

Chapter 32

One Hour Later ...

Although very reluctant, Bobby ordered his assistant to approach Judge Clements with Jeremy's recorded interview and the other material of the case file, to have an arrest warrant secured for his nephew, Seth Kavanaugh. In keeping the stature of being the family man he was, Bobby exercised the only form of leniency he could regarding his nephew. He contacted his brother Woodrow and informed him of the terrible news of what was about to go on with his son. This was a ploy to have the brother be provided a heads up, so he might be able to notify his son of all that was unfolding.

A key component to the whole scenario remained uninspected at this time. Seth's brown Cadillac. The crime took place there. The car was parked at Seth's home. He'd recently bought a new ride. It was a Chevy Corvette. He'd taken that particular vehicle and ridden to the family ranch in the state of Wyoming. Bobby had a hunch that if any heat were to befall any family member of his, let alone Seth, they'd take off in that direction until further notice. This was the protocol in place to avert federal authorities doing their legal alcohol production run. Seth's exit also added to the relief Bobby experienced, being that the nephew was no longer within his arresting jurisdiction, and he could save face in the media by not having to lock him away. The FBI would have to be the ones to do so, then extradite him back to Georgia. Nonetheless, Seth committed a horrendous crime and had to face justice. One way or the other, the law would prevail.

Bobby viewed the case file more.

"I wonder whatever happened to that missing hoop earring?" he questioned himself. *"Maybe it's still inside that Cadillac of his? And I still don't know for the love of my life, how the hell did a nephew of mine become snared in a situation like this? The world may never know."*

***

The search warrant was issued for the search of Seth's property. He was nowhere to be found. However, the Cadillac was. The investigators seized and impounded it. Bobby wasted no time having them sift through the interior of the car, looking to locate a particular piece of evidence, if possible. Small in size but pertinent to the case. The same as those two orange-painted nails. Doctor Turner was wise enough to have collected them at the time he'd plucked them from Seth's body. Whether with the stroke of good luck on the uncle's behalf, or an ass of bad luck on the nephew, either one, was made a reality then and there with the discovery of the 18K gold hoop ornament. It was situated in the deep corner portion of the back seat behind the driver's seat. Bobby was made aware of this fact.

"Well, I be damned!" he thought.

He shook his head in disgust and disbelief over what the nephew had done.

"Why, Seth? Why? All I want to know is . . . why?" Bobby worded in soliloquy. "You didn't have to do what you'd done. But you did. I simply want to know why."

One Week Later . . .

Seth took refuge in Wyoming. He'd been there for four days. He had no plan in place and nowhere to go. The problem wouldn't be going away any time soon. He made an attempt to contact Jeremy. It was learned the friend had been arrested. Jeremy's parents revealed the facts of his situation. They then scolded him beyond any way he'd been bashed in the past. Seth hung up the phone on them, then reached out to his attorney, the particular one he had in mind to retain. Upon being brought to his attention who he was and what he wanted him for, his family name as well, the lawyer respectfully declined to represent him. He then suggested that Seth turned himself into the police. The lawyer then contacted the DA's office there in Savannah and let Bobby know of the exchange. He made him aware of Seth's location, amongst other things. Not that Bobby hadn't come to the conclusion. He only needed confirmation. The FBI was alerted.

Seth thought it was a good idea to call his DA uncle. He wanted to explain his side of the story. Not that it mattered to Bobby.

"Seth. You've gotten yourself in a world of trouble, son. The best thing you could do to help yourself in this ordeal is to turn yourself in. Period!" Bobby said to him.

"Uncle Bobby, I can't do that. Unless you make the situation better for me."

"I can't do that, Seth. I had to step aside and allow a special prosecutor to handle the case to prevent a conflict of interest, due to you being my nephew. I can't have any input on this case. All I want to know from you is why, Seth? Why'd you do it? You couldn't handle being turned down by the Maddox girl? She was a model, Seth, and part of your business. Nothing personal should've interfered with that. Your friend Jeremy has already related everything about what happened. And I subpoenaed your medical files from Doctor Turner. He treated you for two infections. I've got those orange fingernails as well. Your Cadillac was seized. We recovered that missing gold hoop earring from the backseat. Everything we have points squarely at you, Seth. The only good spot you have is that you're presumed innocent until proven guilty in the court of law. So, why won't you do the Kavanaugh family a righteous deed and turn yourself in? It'll be easier on you that way. Besides, I already know where you're hiding out. The federal authorities should be there soon to arrest you. Don't make it any harder than it already is," Bobby responded in a long, drawn-out way.

Seth broke down in tears at that point. He sobbed heavily. Bobby listened in on the emotional meltdown. He picked up a familiar tinkering sound that came from Seth's end.

"Uncle Bobby, I don't have an answer to your questions."

"I have to end this call, Seth. We can't continue to talk. Anything you'd like to say before I do?"

"Yes, sir, Uncle Bobby. There is."

Seth exhaled strongly. He then spoke his peace.

"It'll be over my dead body before I allow myself to be arrested and put on trial for this. That's all I have left to say," Seth stated emphatically.

Click!

Boom!

A powerful gunshot rang out. Bobby heard two separate thuds. Seth had loaded his .357 Magnum, cocked the hammer, and pulled the trigger. The tip of the pistol was pinned to the roof of his mouth. A gaping hole was blown through the top of his head. The weapon and body of Seth hit the floor in the aftermath. Bobby had a good idea about what had taken place. He simply hung up the phone and prepared to receive the official report once the federal agents stormed the place. They were already en route.

***

The dynamic turn of events pushed the case in a different direction. Seth's suicide made the case difficult to prosecute, but not entirely. The primary suspect was dead and couldn't stand trial, but not so the party to the crimes, Jeremy. Bobby felt certain he'd faced many hardships and received a heavy dose of flak in the outcome of it all. A highly publicized and gruesome case wouldn't continue to go unsolved, not prosecuted maybe.

Due to the fact of Jeremy taking his own life by hanging in the jail cell he was locked away in, no one could be punished. He was determined to not take the fall all by himself. At the knowledge of Seth's suicide, Jeremy figured that was the best route for him to take as opposed to the state's executioner having the pleasure to do so. Bobby's focus went towards solving the mysterious disappearance of those two policemen, Flaherty and Carson, being that the story Mickey gave was now disproved in fact and by the evidence of the Maddox case. His attention and anger were now trained on Mickey.

"That goddamn son of a bitch Mickey told me a dog-faced lie. I'm a nail his black ass now! For the old and the new!" Bobby told himself.

He was locked and loaded and ready to roll. The real chase had now begun.

Chapter 33

Several Weeks Later . . .

Johnny Mack and Mickey were together on this day. They wanted to discuss a potential business plan for taking ill-gained money and making legitimate investments. The two were situated inside a second home Mickey was buying. It was a small one, only two bedrooms. Like his first home, he wanted no illegal activities going on there either.

"Never do dirty business where you rest your head," is what he'd always say.

Johnny Mack appeared to be a bit upset about something. Of all people, he had a bone to pick with Mickey and wasted no more time holding back.

"Say, Mickey! You wanna tell me about that phone call between you and my wife?" he asked as they counted money together.

They wrote notes as well.

"If you must be reminded, your wife is my sister in-law and I knew she'd eventually say something to you about it, but the phone conversation... it wasn't nothing serious, Johnny Mack. I only asked a question or two."

"Well…that wasn't how it was reported to me. Natalie said you got huffy with her. What that part be all about?"

"If you must know, Johnny Mack, Josephine took the kids and ran off on me. I asked Natalie where did she run off to? And why would she get in our business and suggest to JoJo to leave me? She had no answers for me. That pissed me off. But I bet she didn't mention nothing like this to you, did she?"

"No. I can't say that she did"

"I'm sure she didn't. But that's not the part we need to be worried about with those two."

He had an alarming tone in his voice. Johnny Mack came to a complete stop with what he was doing and looked on at his cousin with a flare of concern. He knew Mickey well enough to know that there was more to tell him.

"If it's not then what is?"

"It was brought up again by them both. The thing down in Georgia the night we moved up here."

"Get the fuck outta here! Natalie too?"

"Yep. They appear to wanna hold it over our heads, Johnny Mack. This could be a serious problem if we don't get a handle to it quickly," he warned. "They pretty much continue to question things instead of leaving them be. From how Natalie put it, this was one of the main reasons JoJo packed up and hauled ass on me. Something about her level of fear behind it all. It doesn't seem to wanna go away. And that JoJo claimed the need to put some distance between the two of us, at least until everything blows over for good. I'm more than sure Natalie feels about the same way. Only difference is that Natalie didn't actually see any dead bodies. JoJo, on the other hand, did, but she feels the same way. She just won't say it to you."

"You probably right, because not once did she mention anything about JoJo running off on you? And not only that, over the last couple of months, Natalie has brought up how much she missed being home back in Georgia but not able to return now because of the 'situation' that happened and the 'predicament' you and I have put her and her sister in. Shit, Mickey . . . we may do got problems on the horizon."

"May do!" Mickey retorted. "Shit, nigga, we actually do! The real question now becomes, how do we deal with it?"

"We can start by you getting rid of that bitch, Peaches! And then making shit right with your wife all over again. That's what we can do," Johnny Mack gave his raw opinion.

"It ain't that simple, Johnny Mack. And in fact, Peaches is the one person who I know I could use as leverage to make the whole thing go away. She had all the power with her."

"You mind telling me about any of that? All this top secret shit you got going on in the world and I don't know a thing about it. Maybe I can be of good advice. Just maybe. You ever thought of that? And besides, it is because of you how I got drag into this shit to begin with. And it is because of you that I'mma make it my business of my own accord to get the hell out of it. With you or without you, Mickey. And that's the truth." Johnny Mack spoke his peace.

He'd long held those words on his chest and finally found the opportunity to express them. He continued.

"So, get to talking! And don't leave shit out! Because I deserve to know the tall truth."

Mickey had absolutely no choice but to let his cousin know each and every detail that related to the relationship he and Miss Peaches had, along with the business that included Bobby Kavanaugh. He also had to let Johnny Mack know about the plan and place to blackmail Bobby with it if it came to it, regarding their dealings in the underworld they'd done, the pregnancy of Miss Peaches. The two would expose it all to the public so as to sabotage Bobby's marriage and legal career as DA, and a litany of other incriminating activities he would bring to the forefront against Bobby if anything about those two dead cops come knocking at his door in the future.

Once Mickey revealed the information to his cousin, Johnny Mack was stunned to know what all the younger Savage had going on all those years right under his nose.

"Nigga!" Johnny Mack let out. "I just want to know one goddamn thing. How in the hell you got all this high-profile secret society shit going on with these type of folks and I'm now just finding out about it? Just tell me that, will you?"

"It's because… son of my father's brother . . . It wasn't for you to know at the time. The less said is always the best said. There's a time and place for everything. Now what's the time," Mickey stated, putting things in his own way to make it sound good for Johnny Mack.

"There you go, with all that philosophy shit on me! You may got more book sense than I do. But God knows I got way more common sense than you do. Along with the experience. And now that you dragged me into this shit, just make sure that my words are heard, and the input of advice is paid attention to. That's all I ask, bet?"

"Bet!"

"And I'll be sure to get a handle on my wife to be sure she don't utter another word about anything. But truth be told, Natalie never saw the end result of what happened. So technically, she only knows what JoJo has told her. Not an eyewitness to a damn thing. That title belongs to the woman you got in your corner," Johnny Mack pointed out.

"I'm aware of that," responded Mickey. "But it's the woman in your corner, who dictates to the other what to do, being she's the oldest. So, the both of us gotta get a grip on our girls before the man gets a grip on us all. One we won't be able to break free from."

They bumped fists and returned to the business at hand. Not long before, they'd gotten a resupply of heroin. The Italian connection kept the flow steady. The Savage boys had no problem getting rid of the product. However, a disturbing issue began to present itself inside their camp. Hound's body count continued to pile up as he recruited more and more ruthless young thugs to line the of ranks for security of the Black Mafia organization that he and others were building. These dangerous outlaws now had a strict policy that they forced independent dealers to comply with, "to get down or lay down!" The threat was simple and plain to understand, but the consequences for going against that threat proved to hold more weight than anything: that it's always best to be feared whether than loved. Love will get you killed, while fear, it will gain you power.

Chapter 34

Josephine and the kids settled well into the home they now lived in, in Manchester, NH. They'd been enrolled in school and they also cared for the really young ones. JoJo's sister Sasha graduated from school and moved to the North to help her out with the kids. She found work as a housekeeper as well and had a steady income. JoJo properly explained to her why the move was made from Philly to there but excluded the details as to exactly why she wanted to get away from the father of her five kids. She couldn't risk the haunting past to come back and bring harm to them. JoJo also didn't know whether or not her sister was able to hold water.

The wife of Mickey Savage was now a full-grown woman in all her wiles and ways, not just based on the fact of giving birth to five kids. Her boss lady, Mrs. Hammock, had properly taught her the correct etiquette of how she was to behave in public, how to modestly style and dress herself, how to correctly pamper and apply makeup, how to speak proper English and articulate, and the basics of leg-crossing. Everything that Mrs. Hammock taught JoJo was to benefit her and help grow the business she owned and operated.

Communication and perception were very important in the line of work Mrs. Hammock thrived in. Clients needed to trust them well enough to welcome them into their homes. With JoJo being a black woman in those times who dressed like a white woman, straightened her hair like one, and happened to speak in the same way one would, the job done on her by her employer truly was on display. JoJo was grateful for it. Mrs. Hammock had a sister named Diane. She also embraced JoJo as a friend and became hands on with the young lady in terms of economics, the cooking and dietary area primarily.

Mrs. Diane Prather had his son named Winston. He took notice of JoJo at his aunt's home and shop. He'd heard of her on numerous occasions prior to her move to New Hampshire and now had the pleasure of seeing her live in person. He became attracted to the smooth soot complexioned beauty that had unique facial features, and desired to date her, if she was willing. Winston wanted to exclusively communicate to JoJo how much he took a liking to her. He made it his business to lounge around the decor shop JoJo and his mother ran for Mrs. Hammock.

Over time, an acquaintance was developed between Winston and JoJo. They began to talk daily. He was finally able to convince JoJo out on a date. This may would have taken place sooner if JoJo wasn't so fearful of being out in public as a black woman with a white man, although the threat was more so against a black male being exposed in public with a white woman. It took JoJo a lot of time to rid herself of the fear and eventually she was without it. Racial issues in the North weren't as bad as that of the South. Especially not so with New Hampshire in comparison to Georgia.

Their first time out, the two enjoyed dinner and a movie. Winston took the opportunity to get to know JoJo more personally. She opened up to him with ease.

"So, tell me a few things about you personally, Josephine, if you will?" Winston asked.

"What is it in particular you like to know?" she responded.

"Where you from originally?"

"I'm a southern girl. Georgia is my home state."

"Oh, okay. You don't have a southern accent. I wouldn't have ever known."

"Yeah. I moved to Philadelphia in 1958. Over time, I managed to get rid of my country tongue."

"Understood, so you move up north on your own or with family?"

"With my husband," she replied.

There was a level of reluctance in her voice at the mention of her spouse.

"With your husband!" he retorted.

He was taken aback by the revelation. "I wouldn't have never known you'd tied the knot before."

"I'm still married. We're just separated for the time being."

"For the time being, huh? Any kids?"

"Yeah, I have kids. Five to be exact."

"Five! My Lord, your husband kept you busy, didn't he!" he let out.

JoJo smiled behind his reaction.

"So, I guess you're not as interested now as you were before I made you aware of my many children, are you?" Her instincts pushed her to state the obvious.

"I can't say that I'm not. You're a very beautiful woman, Josephine. Polished. Well-spoken and well-mannered. And atop of that, you've lived life in the correct way before the eyes of God. Your kids were born through wedlock. And you've maintained well. Therefore, my interest level is still there based upon those facts. But you mind me asking the reason for the separation?"

"It's a long story. I'd rather not have my night with you ruined behind the thought. But what about you? Wanna fill me in on what I don't already know?"

"Do I wanna fill you in on what you don't already know about me, you ask? What has my mother and aunt shared with you so far?"

"Everything I needed to know before I agreed to this date. I did my homework. The same way you had been checking for me... I was busy checking for you. Life is all about there being and even exchange when it comes to the opposite sexes, Sir Winston Prather," she said unto him in her own catchy way.

JoJo displayed a level of knowledge in philosophy she'd learned. Winston was caused to smile.

"Well . . . as you may or may not know, I graduated Penn University with a master's degree in banking and financial management. Like you, I've been married. I have two kids with my now ex-wife due to our divorce. And I'm thirty years of age. I'm single and looking to meet someone who I'm able to get along with, marry again at some point, and make more babies. I'm very independent and financially situated. I'm on the path to being a rich and powerful man in the world, and I would like to know how may I continue to cater to you, my dear?"

Winston poured on his charm and wits. JoJo blushed as never before. She had no idea that a white guy could have the same type of gift-of-gab as a black guy could. But then again, she'd never been involved in an intimate setting with a white guy either, so the experience was totally new. It felt good to her as well.

"What is it about me that interest you so much, Winston? Other than what you've said so far?"

He smiled mischievously at her works. The glints of his eyes intensified in illumination. He appeared delighted at the chance to give an answer to the particular question.

"You really wanna hear my response to that? I would've thought it was obvious by now."

JoJo produced a smile of her own to match his.

"I asked, didn't I," she said now up closer to his face as if they were about to kiss.

"Josephine . . . honestly… a white male like myself holds the same burning desire to have a sexual encounter with a black female, much like black males hold for white women, if not more. It's the same difference, but for me, I take a liking to you more than a sexual attraction. I love the way your mind functions. You're not afraid to embrace a different culture. And you're a well-read female. I believe we'd make a beautiful couple."

He expressed himself to the best of his abilities. The question was now would JoJo go for him? She looked on at him while still holding a smile.

"I believe we would too. You just gotta add a little more bad boy-ism to yourself. Present more swagger to your style and demeanor."

Winston was made aware of a she favored about the character of a man.

"So, you'd like for me to incorporate some ruggedness to who I am?"

"Not much. Just a touch of toughness because we could be in for a helluva lot of criticism from people who don't agree with interracial couples. That's why I say that."

"I agree. And the toughness part is already there. I was a wild dude during my days in college. A party animal, no doubt."

They both smiled behind his comment.

"I bet you were, you spoiled brat you," JoJo said then reach over and pinch him on the cheek.

She planted a kiss there as well. The interracial duo completed their meals and made way to the movie theater at that point. At the time, there was a recent flick out by Sir Alfred Hitchcock that created a buzz. Winston and JoJo had a really good time on the first date out. More of the same was on the agenda in future plans. The chemistry couldn't be denied.

Chapter 35

Miss Peaches made it her business to contact Bobby Kavanaugh to relate to him the progress in pregnancy she was experiencing. She was now nearly seven months into it, and it showed. Bobby had long expressed anger at himself for placing an emphasis on personal pleasure and becoming trapped in the situation he was in with Peaches. Had he remained locked in and focused on his career as a judicial official, there would be no mess to sort out, but he failed to do so. And at all costs, he needed to prevent his infidelities and activities from leaking to the public. Such scandal could potentially ruin him as a man and professional figure. He'd be doomed if either of the two had.

Peaches wanted to at least hear his voice and say hello. Bobby had a private line they communicated through.

"Bobby here," he answered, not exactly knowing who it was.

"Hey, Bobby. How are you?"

"Evelyn?" He recognized the voice.

"Yeah, it's me," she responded.

"I'm doing alright. What about you?"

"I'm making it. Just a few months left before my due date. I can't wait to have your baby. I really can't."

"Is that so? How come I'm just now hearing from you? It's been months, Evelyn."

"I'm away, Bobby. Still visiting with family. When I have the baby, I'll be sure to come see you then. But right now, I can't."

"Well, how come you can't?" Bobby wanted to know. "I miss you."

"To be totally honest with you, Bobby, I'm afraid. I really am."

"You're afraid of what?"

"I'm paranoid and suffer from bouts of anxiety. And I don't have a clue of what you may potentially do to me or this baby of yours I'm carrying. It's nineteen sixty-five, Bobby. There are a lot of people from your side of the tracks that hate the idea that the Civil Rights Bill got passed into law to allow black people to have some rights that white people fight like all hell to keep them away from. And to—"

"What does that have to do with you and me, Evelyn?" Bobby cut her words short to say.

"It has a lot to do with us, Bobby. You're a very powerful man. One who has authority and rule over other powerful men. Powerful white men, Bobby! How do you think these other men would take it if they were to find out you impregnated a black female? And atop that, you're a married man. You got a family. Our affair could ruin your career, your marriage, or potentially your life. And I'm sure before you would allow that to happen, you'd kill my black ass dead! This damn baby too! If you had to eliminate the threat to your positions in life." Miss Peaches spoke on her state of mind. The reality she feared the most.

"Let's not be ridiculous here, Evelyn. Now you know I wouldn't do such a thing like that. I wouldn't do nothing in the world to harm you. I love you, gal. And you know I do."

"If that be truth, then why haven't you situated me into a place of my own? A nice home where I can raise our child peacefully? My baby is gonna bear your namesake, Bobby. He or she will be a Kavanaugh."

"Now you hold on there, Evelyn! You jumping the gun a little bit there, aren't you? I should have some input on whether or not that baby should be a Kavanaugh or not, shouldn't I? I may want the baby to carry on your family's name," Bobby detested.

"Now you see what I mean there, Bobby? This is your baby. One you put inside me. Why wouldn't you want the baby to be a Kavanaugh? Your other two kids are. Why not the one I'm to have?"

"Evelyn, we need to have a conversation in person. How soon could you get here to Georgia?"

"Bobby, that won't be happening under no circumstances. I told you I'm too afraid to be alone with you. And when I finally do drop this load, me and the baby won't be either. I'll probably agree to meet you by myself somewhere in public, but I can't allow you the chance to kill us both at one time. That's not gonna happen, but what you could do is at the next available break you get, we could meet down in Miami again and have a talk. That way, we won't be on your territory, and I'll feel safe. Now how does that sound?" Peaches asked.

"We can do just that in about two to three weeks, give or take. We certainly can."

"And your ol' pal, Mickey. He gonna be there with me too. He says you two need to talk. That y'all haven't done so in quite a while."

"Now that, we do. If he hasn't heard by now, I've got news to share with him."

"I'll be sure to let him know. Also, I need travel money, Bobby. And funds to carry me through with this baby. How soon could you wire me something?"

"I need an address or a post box number. I'll send a money order or two," Bobby declared.

"I'll get back with you tomorrow on that, okay? And you take care, Bobby. You hear?"

"You do the same Evelyn."

The call came to an end. Mickey and Sparkle looked at Miss Peaches the entire time she had Bobby on the phone. The three were situated in Mickey's second home, the Safehouse, he liked to call it.

"I wonder what news Bobby has he wants to share with me?" Mickey questioned.

He then picked up the phone to contact a family member of his brother Otis, down in Savannah. Otis relayed to Mickey everything that the news station had out about the Norma Maddox case and the suicide deaths related to it of Seth and Jeremy. Mickey had Otis to go out and buy all the Savannah morning newspapers that headlined or included the story. He wanted them mailed to him and desired to read all about it for himself, so he'd know the full extent of all that took place in his absence. Otis did what he asked, and the two brothers thanked one another.

One Day Later . . .

Miss Peaches contacted Bobby once more, but this time to provide him with a Post Office box number to a New Jersey location. Mickey had her travel across the bridge to Camden to open one. He didn't want or need for Bobby to get hot on the trail with any knowledge about Philadelphia. Bobby proved good at speculating, and Mickey didn't want him knowing a thing about he and Miss Peaches being in close proximity.

There also was the intention to call Bobby himself to know what he wanted to speak with him about. Passing up on that, Mickey concluded that it was simply best to wait until they were in Miami again. That way they could go over everything in person. Besides, the trip for them all would be at Bobby's expense, via the money orders he was to send Peaches, his caramel-complexioned mistress.

Chapter 36

After being made aware of the danger that JoJo and Natalie posed upon them by Mickey, Johnny Mack definitely wanted to have a conversation with his wife so as to get a handle on the situation and relate to her what he now knew. His attention was to poke at the idea with his words about the three of them coming together to talk over everything. He'd know for himself from that point the severity of the threat, being he always felt that Natalie was more on her sister's side than she was his. Husband or not. They were alone at home on this day, a Thursday afternoon. The kids were in school.

Johnny Mack initiated the talk.

"Natalie, how about I had a conversation with Mickey, and he mentioned to me exactly how the phone call went between the both of you?"

"What you mean he mentioned to you 'exactly' how the phone call went between the both of us?" she retorted.

The mention of Mickey's name brought a scornful look about her face.

"So, what, my words wasn't good enough for you?"

"You left out a few things. And with me being your husband, I don't need you finding your way into them folks' business anymore, okay? Let them have that. And we have ours. Two totally set of problems that's different from one another."

"Johnny Mack, to be honest with you, you're my husband and all, and I respect you. But as it applies to this situation, I don't give a damn what you say! My sister's problems are always gonna be my problems. And anytime she gives me a call about something like she did, I'm gonna give her the best advice I know on how to deal with those problems. And not only that, I didn't leave out anything with what I said to you. I told you all you needed to know on that particular subject."

At no time in their relationship had Natalie appeared to be rebellious and back talk at Johnny Mack. He was taken by surprise behind her behavior. He looked at her with squinted eyes and anger about his face.

"Natalie, why did you put the idea in your sister's head for her to up and leave the man? Their business is none of your business. And why did you keep the part from me about JoJo bringing up the past about what happened in their house down in Georgia?" he stated emphatically. "That's what I would like to know."

"All I know is whatever happened in that house that night has made it to where we can't even go home. Not even to visit like we want to. And my sister is terrified out of her ever-loving mind!" Natalie got louder with her words.

"Don't be acting like JoJo ain't never mentioned anything to you because I know she has."

"You're right, she has and she's scared that the police is going to someday arrest her too behind the incident and give her life in prison... after they give Mickey the goddamn electric chair! We ain't have shit to do with what you and that sneaky ass, no-good cousin of yours has done, and now we got to keep hid for the rest of your lives! And why he seem to be concerned about JoJo leaving him? Don't he got some other woman named Peaches to keep him busy? JoJo now doing so much better without him. Tell him to get over it, won't you!" Natalie barked at him.

"Natalie, mind your own goddamn business, you hear! And you keep your fucking mouth closed about anything that took place back then, I'm telling you!" Johnny Mack warned.

"And if I don't, what!" she challenged with further back talk. "Hell, it might even be a good idea for me and JoJo to take a trip down south to Georgia, and she clear her name by telling the police all that she saw and what she know!"

Natalie's threat was more serious than Johnny Mack originally thought. Why would she go against him like that? He reacted violently.

Whop!

Down to the floor Natalie went. Johnny Mack smacked the fuck out of her. He then leaned over her while she lay on the floor and holding the left side of her face.

"It might be a good idea to do what? Say that shit again!" he yelled and pulled her arm out the way to prevent blocking.

Whop!

Then again.

"Go on! Say it one more time!"

Whop!

He continued holding her arm and smacking her silly.

"Why you won't say it again? I wanna hear you say it one more time. It might be a good idea to willingly snitch to the police on me and my people! Is that what you said?"

Whop!

"Huh?"

Whop . . . Whop!

"Now fucking apologize before I knock hell out you again! But this time, with my goddamn fist! What the fuck

160

wrong with you, Natalie? I would've thought you know better!"

"I'm sorry, Johnny Mack. I'm sorry, baby. I won't say something like that again, okay? I promise. I'm sorry, sweetheart."

"Good! Now get your ass up and go in there to the kitchen and cook so me and the kids can eat when they come home! And keep your fucking nose outta Mickey and JoJo's business! It don't concern you or me!" he spat.

Johnny Mack grabbed his jacket and his hat and left out the house to have a cool-off period from the high level of anger he'd felt.

"She talking about snitching on a motherfucker! I ain't marry and have no goddamn kids by a rat! What the fuck wrong with her!" he said aloud to himself.

He couldn't believe Natalie would say such a thing like that. He'd never laid a hand on her up until that day. This was only the beginning of the problems that were to potentially come the way of Johnny Mack and Mickey behind their dark secret. There would be a lot to deal with.

Chapter 37

Hound Savage became very active in the business of extortion and execution. He had the murder game pinned under his thumb and turned the screw to it when and how he saw fit. He felt as though he couldn't be stopped. Not by the cops. Not by any rivalry black crew. Not by the mafia. Not by anybody. And to add a reinforcement to the power his security team had, he added a guy to the ranks who'd not long been dishonorably discharged out of the Army. The new Black Mafia member was a former guard over the main weapon armory located in Texas and knew the in and out routes on how to steal artillery from the place, if and when he chose to.

Frank Brown had a serious grudge now against the American government and also the military in particular, behind the failed invasion of the Bay of the Pigs in Cuba that almost cost him his own life, but actually claimed the lives of several black comrades who he had much love for. At all costs, Frank sought vengeance against the political system. He desired to kill white cops, white politicians, and white judicial officials. Also included were Negroes whom he deemed "worthless," and those of the blacks who sided with "white" (or Whitey). To put it simply, Frank was the black militant that was eager for action.

While Mickey was away on other business, the duty was on Hound and Johnny Mack to oversee and run their heroin operation. Hound and his ruthless cohorts worked the trenches, getting their hands dirty while Johnny Mack covered the higher end of things and situated the money. Hound would never be the one to pass up the opportunity to pull off a high stakes caper. He was provided a tip from an Italian partner of his regarding another Italian rival that had a stash house they utilized to keep kilos of heroin and plenty of money.

The place belonged to the brother of a very powerful man in the underworld and beyond. He was Angelo Marconi, the head man and don of the Marconi crime family, a syndicate that be bears his namesake. Angelo was the supplier to the Savage cousins, but only dealt with Mickey with his heroin product. His brother, Peter, owned the home where the narcotics were tucked away. Peter and his wife of many years, along with their beloved poodle, Kathy.

The Scalia Family associate, a guy by the name of Neil, wasn't a made man as of yet. He was seeking to be, putting in heavy work to appease the Scalia Mafia top men to finally let him make his bones and be initiated. His tip to Hound was that he had it on good authority that there was at least fifty or more kilos grade-A smack put away in the home someplace. And that, once the job is completed, he only wanted ten of them for his information. Neil even made it his business to show Hound the location of the home, in an area out from the Philly limits, in Westchester, Pennsylvania.

The old man, Peter, occasionally kept a security man on hand to protect him and his wife. You just never know, in the world of the mafia, but oftentimes it's only him, his wife and the dog. An easy mission if they were to strike while

Peter was away. No matter how hard he tried to resist the temptation, Hound simply had to agree to do the dirty deed and go out to see what he and his boys might be able to come away with. There was an advantage to it as well for Hound. He knew exactly who the old man Peter was and what he looked like. Peter was there at the pool hall in South Philly the day he, Mickey and Johnny Mack became connected with the Marconi family in business, and also the times that followed. Each deal that went on, Peter was onsite to oversee the transaction.

Hound and two of his most trusted Black Mafia brethren set out to accomplish the mission at hand, the home invasion of Peter Marconi. There was a wooded area surrounding the house. A safe spot to take cover and spy on the place before striking. Neil told Hound that the best time to take action with between 3:00 and 7:00 P.M., the portion of the day when Peter would always be in Philly with the crew. He was the underboss. A perfect plan was put in play by Hound for things to go smoothly. It was he, Frank and Lacy.

Just before the crack of dawn on the day the caper was to happen, Hound and his soldiers found a spot in the woods near the home to park the getaway vehicle. On the days leading up, they'd scouted out the area and the roadways surrounding. Now on location, they eased closer to the bushes nearest the home to lie and wait for Peter to leave. Some days he'd drive, but most often, a Marconi soldier would pick him up to be taken to the pool hall social club.

Frank, the more learned of the three in these types of matters, brought along a pair of binoculars as well, to have a closer look in on the house and the yard. They had no problems waiting nine hours or more for the type of contraband they aimed to get. Fifty or more kilos were worth it. The time reached 1:00 P.M. The robbery trio was still lying low in the bush with their focus locked in on the front of the house at the eighty-yard distance it sat.

"We ain't got too much longer, huh Hound?" stated Lacy. "The little old lady will be home all alone at that point, and then we can go in easily to take those fresh baked cookies she keep a watch over for the husband while he's away."

Lacy caused them all to have a laugh behind his comment.

"You got that part right! But the other part, you got wrong," Hound responded.

"What part wrong?"

"The 'home alone' part," Hound made him aware.

Lacy looked at him with an expression of confusion. Hound went on to clarify what he meant.

"You must've forgot, the old guinea bitch got a fucking dog. I was told that she takes care of like it's a muthafuckin' human!"

The wise crack caused more laughter.

"A goddamn poodle at that! A little furry white poodle!" Hound said further.

Nearly twenty minutes later, a black Lincoln Town Car pulled up the long driveway and headed towards the house.

"They must be picking the old geezer up early today," Frank let out.

The sudden turn of Peter's time schedule had them scratching their heads for a moment, but nothing too much to be concerned over to have a change of plans.

"Must be," responded Hound. "Take a good look, Frank, and see what's going on," he instructed.

Frank put the binoculars to his eyes to be made aware of how many, and who specifically.

"Only one in the car. A younger hood with slick hair. He must be the pick-up man for ol' Pete," Frank informed.

Hound then got the binoculars from Frank and had a look to confirm that indeed it was Peter, and he was leaving for the day. He exited the house, got into the car, and the two rode away with no one behind but the wife, the dog, and the main thing the black thieves came for, the narcotics. Hound and company gave a twenty-minute pause before finally making their move. They had to ensure that Peter hadn't forgotten something and needed to return home.

The three trotted along the wooded lining that surrounded the two-story house. They reached the backyard and took notice of the sliding glass door to the ground level patio. The old lady was spotted inside the house pacing through the dining room. She had on an apron and appeared to be preparing to do gardening work or something in the floral department. She had on a large hat too, one of those dark brown cloth headpieces to protect her from the sun. It was the month of March. The heat was on its way. The estate had a mini greenhouse in the backyard. The bandits noticed it.

"This shit may be easier than I originally thought," Hound remarked.

He put two and two together and guessed that the old lady was about to come out the house and go to the greenhouse to do work.

"Damn sure look that way," Frank chimed in to say upon observing what Hound concluded.

Peter's wife appeared at the back door. The glass slid open.

"Come on, Kathy. Let's go, girl," she called out for her dog.

The pet detected something strange through her senses. She became reluctant to exit the house, moving slowly and pausing in the process.

"Arf! Arf! Arf! Arf!"

The poodle barked at a high pitch. Her sense of smell picked up something out of the ordinary. The old lady and her dog had done this many times. Therefore, she thought nothing too much of it and felt that the dog was simply misbehaving, as she was at moments prone to doing.

"What's wrong with you today, baby? You okay?" The fiery frail Mrs. this spoke to the dog as if she was an actual human being.

The dog stood motionless and looked at its owner.

"Arf! Arf!" Kathy barked more.

"Kathy! Come on now, will you? Let's get some work done, baby."

The dog still didn't move.

"You know what," the owner worded, then reached down to grab the dog in effort to carry her to the greenhouse destination.

At that point, Hound and the boys made their move. The three men rushed the woman and the dog in ambush. Before the lady was able to turn around, they were upon her.

"Arf-Arf-Arf-Arf!" Kathy barked vehemently.

"Come here you two bitches!" Hound spat from behind his ski-mask through gritted teeth.

He gripped the old lady around the neck in a violent chokehold from behind. Lacy was the one who grabbed the noisy dog by both hind legs then slammed Kathy without mercy to the hard cement of the patio, cracking the skull of the canine and knocking her out, nearly killing the beloved pet. Hound let off with the brute pressure he had around the old lady's throat. He had no intentions to kill her. He needed her to talk and tell them where the dope was located.

Chapter 38

They dragged her inside the house. Frank and Lacy were responsible for making a quick run through each room with their pistols drawn to be sure no one else was there. They made a shocking discovery on the second level of the house. There was another elderly lady in the room and seated in the recliner in front of a TV. She had on a mask that was attached to a tube that led to her oxygen tank. Apparently, the woman had a breathing issue. Her respiratory system was a wreck. Probably a bad case of emphysema.

Frank yanked the mask from her face and pushed her over onto the floor and proceeded to tie up the poor-health-having woman. Her ankles first, then her wrists behind her back. He dragged her from the room, down the stairs, and through the kitchen floor where Hound had the other woman now bound tightly and gagged, along with the dog. Turned out the two women were sisters. The one with the breathing problem began gasping for air frantically.

"This what I found upstairs in one of the bedrooms, Hound," Frank informed.

"What the fuck seems to be wrong with her? This bitch going through it, ain't she?" Hound let out in response.

"The bitch was on some type of air tank, bro," Frank informed.

"Oh, well! What the fuck! It wasn't her day to breathe easy, now was it!" Hound remarked and shrugged his shoulders at the same time.

Peter's wife, Sylvia, now began to come around from the moment of briefly blacking out.

"What you people want? And where is my dog? Kathy! Come to mommy, girl," she called out for her pet. "Huh! Oh my God! What have you all done!"

She then yelped upon notice that they had her disabled sibling tied up next to her.

"My sister is gonna die if she doesn't get her oxygen tank immediately! Do you buffoons have any knowledge of who I'm the wife of, or who my husband's brother is?" Sylvia yelled.

"Obviously, we do! That's why we're here! And that goddamn sister of yours and the piece of shit mutt there, not gonna be the only two to die if you don't tell us where that husband of yours has the dope stashed at!" Hound issued a strong ultimatum.

He lowered the gag further for her to clearly speak. Sylvia noticed the large blood stain on Kathy's head.

"What have you done to my baby!" she wailed in grief over the dog.

The poodle wasn't the only problem. Her sister was now barely breathing.

"I tell you what! Maybe a nice oven roasted doggie will make you talk faster!" Hound threatened.

Sylvia was made aware that the intruders were all black guys.

"You damn niggers!!! Angelo is gonna have y'all asses, you hear!!!" she returned fire with fire.

Hound looked from Frank to Lacy and smiled at what the old lady had said. His teeth showed vividly on display.

"I think this bitch got the wrong impression like we bullshittin' or something," he said. "Show this bitch that we for real, bro!"

That was code to Lacy for him to do something drastic.

"Take that fuckin' mutt and toss that bitch in the oven," Hound ordered.

Lacy jumped to the occasion. He grabbed the dog by the hind legs once again and raced to the stove. Sylvia already had a roast cooking and the heat was already at a high degree. Lacy put on a mitten, pulled the meat pan out and sat it on the floor. At that point, he took Kathy by her neck, pinned her to the floor, poured barbecue sauce and ketchup onto the helpless animal, and threw the dog into the oven without a drop of remorse.

"Now . . . You next, bitch, if you don't get to talking!" spat Hound.

Sylvia began to cry as never before over her beloved Kathy. Words couldn't describe the degree of grief she experienced at the sound of the dog bellowing for help.

Whop!

Hound slapped Sylvia viciously about the face.

"Now talk, bitch! I want to know, where is that fucking heroin at? And I want to know now!"

"Please! Please! Don't kill me! Whatever it is you're looking for, my husband has a vault behind the bookshelf there in the living room. Take it! Take it all! Everything that's inside. Then leave!" Sylvia said.

Hound looked towards the other two and gave a heads-up motion. Frank and Lacy fast-stepped to the front room and together pushed the large bookcase over onto the floor though it did have a rolling wheel railing to it. Books scattered all over the place. The door to the vault had wallpaper to cover it. They ripped it off. A latch handle through the door appeared. No locks. Frank pushed down on it to open the twenty-four by thirty-six-inch door. He and Lacy looked at the triple layer rows of kilos well situated within. In addition, there was ninety thousand in cash and four pistols, two automatics and two revolvers.

The old man Peter was a tad senile to a degree. He kept a mini address book style journal there in the vault as well. It had a lot of important information in it to help him keep up with business. He never fathomed a home invasion being carried out on him and his wife. Peter operated in the same fashion for thirty years or so. Only, heroin was the new wave of contraband he kept.

"Hell, yeah. Blue tick! We gotta hit! It's what we're here for. And extras!" Frank let out.

Lacy ran up the steps to go and grab a couple of bed sheets and return. He and Frank pulled each brick of heroin one by one from the vault that was converted from a fireplace. The space was about six feet inward.

"We got eighty in all, my guy!" Lacy yelled out to Hound.

He was ecstatic. Hound still had a knee pinned onto the old lady's neck. Smoke from the dog cooking began to come out the oven and blanket the kitchen, but for the most part, the heat vent provided a way for the hazardous material to be freed. Sylvia's sibling was now dead. Lack of proper oxygen killed her. Sylvia was the only one still allowed to live.

"Eighty kilos in all, ninety large ones in cash, and these beauties," Frank made mention to Hound and showcased the spoils of war.

"Goddamn! That vault was big enough to hold all that shit?" Hound let out in surprise.

"That muthafucka' does have a little size to it. But the best part about it was that for it to be a vault, and holding all that shit inside, there wasn't any kind of lock to it. And we walk away with this here too," Lacy said, then presented Hound with the address book that came with the rest of the material they was taking. "How sweet it is, ain't it, Hound?" He smiled happily, showing teeth.

Hound managed to catch onto the slip-up Lacy made at the mention of his name. He brushed it off as nothing and figured that Sylvia was just as senile as her husband was, and didn't comprehend anything. He then gripped Sylvia by her long gray hair and demanded more.

"Where the fuck are the keys to that car out front?"

She indicated with her head in the direction of the front door. The three intruders all looked one way. A key ring holder hung beside the wooden door.

"Take the keys and pull the car to the back of the house, bro," Hound instructed Lacy.

He went off to do his duty. Sylvia started to cry again, but this time in a more intense fashion. More agonizing than before, she knew without a doubt that her sister had died, and her dog was burned to an ash. The remainder of her life would be a paranoid wreck behind the robbery. There would be no more such thing as normal life for Sylvia and her family from that day forward.

"Now we want you to have a blessed remainder if your day, ma'am, okay? Take care!" Hound taunted, then pressed her face hard onto the floor.

He broke her nose throughout the moment. Sylvia just lay there and didn't move, only sobbed more. Blood oozed from the split suffered on the bridge of her nose. Hound and Frank exited the back door with the goods tied tightly in a knapsack. They tossed everything into the backseat of Peter and Sylvia's Lincoln that they were taking as well. The trio vacated the premises, enroute to the getaway car they had hiding in the woods about a mile away.

Nearly an hour later, they made it back to Philly safe and sound with the material. The mafia family Peter belonged to would become very pissed behind the actions perpetrated against them by Hound and crew. They were going to want blood and vengeance. Somebody would have to pay, and based on the fact that Sylvia knew that the intruders were black, the flood gates of fire and fury would open and be directed at any and all the "jungle bunnies" that Peter, Angelo, or any of the highly ranked Marconi family suspected of having anything to do with it or knew something about it.

There was an in-law dead, a beloved pet torched in the oven, a wife assaulted and now traumatized, and product, money, and weapons taken. Who in the hell in their correct minds had the balls and the audacity to disrespect and rob the top Italian mafia family of Philly? The answer to that would be a bold and brazen new nemesis in town that called themselves the Black Mafia Family! Everybody else outside of that had to "get down or lay down!" Who the fuck wanted what! It was the beginning of a takeover. The city of Philly was about to feel it!

Chapter 39

The time was at hand for Bobby to meet up with Miss Peaches and Mickey down in Miami again. Peaches and Mickey took the trip by train a day prior and awaited Bobby. He had a personal driver make the journey with him, an assistant who was also a friend. Grover was his name. The two had known one another since their days as youths.

Everyone checked into the same hotel. It was the Tropical Inn. Bobby had a suite on the second floor, while Miss Peaches and Mickey reserved separate rooms on the fourth floor. Sparkle was invited to join as well. Peaches asked Bobby to visit her in her suite, and to come alone. He mentioned Grover's presence. Once settled in, Bobby made his way to see Miss Peaches. He tapped on the door and was allowed inside. Peaches closed the door, and they greeted one another.

"Hey, Bobby! How you been?" she asked.

Her belly bulged behind the thin material maternity clothing she had on.

"I'm well, Evelyn. What about you?" he responded.

A sense of compassion passed through him at the sight of her pregnancy. This was the first time they'd seen one another since she'd been with child. The two hugged and briefly kissed. Bobby began a walk-through of the suite to check and be sure it was only he and Peaches. He stopped at the closet first. No one was there. He turned and made a trek to the bathroom. Peaches caused him to stop before he made it to the door.

"Bobby! The only other person here with us is . . . Mickey, your friend."

This was Mickey's cue to come out of hiding. He opened the door to the bathroom and was met by Bobby.

"How you been, Bobby?" Mickey greeted.

"Great! What about you, Mickey?" he responded.

"I've been making it. This crazy life I live. Nonetheless, I'm glad to see you, buddy. Miss Peaches told me you wanted to talk. That you had something of importance to speak with me about. So, I came to the conclusion that we could all meet up again at one time, as we are now."

"Good thinking ahead on your behalf, but my intention was to meet you both individually, beginning with Evelyn first."

"—But we are here now," Mickey quickly cut in to say.

"You're correct, so we may as well get to it. Shall we?" replied Bobby.

He walked over to the table and took a seat on one of the chairs. Mickey did the same. Peaches sat atop the bed on the edge of the mattress. There was a stack of newspapers situated atop of the table. Mickey placed them there. He sifted through them for specific ones. He then spoke out.

So, I'm guessing that the way things played out with your nephew clears me as a potential suspect in the Maddox girl case, doesn't it?" he asked, causing Peaches to give him a look of confusion. She needed to now listen closely to know what they were talking about.

"I would assume it should, and this was one of the main things I felt the need to speak with you about, to notify you that a mishap occurred by your name wrongly being mentioned through the investigation somehow. My apologies to you."

"Apologies, accepted. I'm just glad to know that the truth behind the matter eventually came to the light. I just wouldn't have ever thought Seth to be—"

"Hey, hey, hey, there, Mickey!" Bobby, cut in to say. "That's enough. It's over, we can move forward."

"Absolutely, we can. How may we be of service to one another again as we move forward?"

"I have to think over that one there. I'm a man of superior judicial influence now and had to put away the old business ventures once explored. The law doesn't see color. It only sees those who observe it, and deals with those who break it. And in my department that means… that mean I'm responsible for putting bad guys and gals away wheresoever they should be. Simple and plain, my friend."

"Well, when it comes to that, you know I've always been on the opposite side of the law. Bobby, I have zero intentions to line myself up with it as opposed to you. I'm a reluctant one to the rule of law. A Savage by name and nature, and I once knew you to be the way that I am… doing the things that I do. Isn't that how the Kavanaugh family made their fortune? It's just too bad now that the partnership we once shared is no more. We now operate on two different philosophies and I'm sure you won't hesitate now to prosecute my black ass if I were to break any laws on your watch."

"For me to prosecute you in court of law, you would have to do something in the jurisdiction I'm over. Unless you've already done something in your past. To be honest, I don't think you'd be the type of fella to all of a sudden turn and get sloppy in your underworld affairs, if you ever decide to move back to Savannah from Philadelphia," Bobby stated.

Chapter 40

Mickey jarred his head at Bobby's words. He was shocked to know that the prosecutor had learned his current city of residence.

"How do you come to the conclusion that I now live in Philadelphia, Bobby?" he asked. "I never shared that with you."

"You didn't have to share it with me for it to be known. I'm a District Attorney, you forgot? I have power and resources galore," countered Bobby. He palmed a .22 caliber Derringer in his pocket at the same time.

Mickey looked at him. The two held strong eye contact. Tension developed. Miss Peaches looked from one to the other in observance as each spoke. Bobby had more to say.

"And what I'm gonna need for you to do is place your goddamn hands where I can see them, Methuselah Savage!" Bobby declared in a loud voice and drew the pistol. "Mickey Savage, I'm about to contact the police and have you arrested for transport back to Georgia for the murder and concealing of the deaths of two Savannah policemen a few years back!"

"Bobby! What are you doing?" Miss Peaches yelled out.

This was the thing Mickey needed for him to make a quick reaction. Bobby briefly turned his head from Mickey to Peaches and trained the gun on her, then back at Mickey.

"The both of you are now under arrest, so keep your hands where I can see them!" Bobby ordered, waving the gun from one to the other.

"Peaches, get him!" shouted Mickey.

He then grabbed the stack of newspapers and threw them at Bobby.

Pow!

Bobby fired a shot in Mickey's direction. He then turned to face Peaches once more.

Pow!

He fired a second round while aiming at her. He intentionally tried to shoot her in the belly to terminate the baby she carried, growing inside. Bobby wanted the baby dead. Now out of bullets, he tried to load two more quickly. Mickey grabbed the lamp closest to the bed on the nightstand and slung it at Bobby. He made a break towards the window. It led to the balcony. He took a dive with both hands situated over his head and arms crossed and locked.

Upon contact with the thick glass, Mickey crashed through it with his two-hundred-plus-pound body. Shattered pieces of large glass shards were all about the floor. He landed on the concrete of the platform, got to his feet, made another quick scramble toward the railing's fire escape, and rapidly let himself down, one level at a time. He then disappeared into the darkness at the Florida night. Mickey wasn't armed.

Bobby turned to have a look at Peaches. She'd fallen backwards onto the bed. Her back and neck were against the headboard. She had her mouth wide, and her eyes were flooded with tears. There was a large bloodstain on her blouse from the gunshot wound.

***

"Bobby, you shot me!" she let out in a painful voice. "You shot me, Bobby. Why?" she panted with her words.

It became difficult for her to speak. Peaches blacked out at that point. Bobby ran out of the room and headed down the stairs to the front desk of the lobby. He had the clerk call the police and an ambulance. There was no way he could do one and leave out the other. His story had to be in order by the time the cops arrived, or it wouldn't fly over so well.

The Miami police and medical personnel made it to the scene some twenty minutes later. What Bobby told them was that Methuselah Savage—a suspect and person of interest to the Savannah Police regarding two cops feared dead—wanted to speak with him about the events that unfolded at his residence the night the policeman disappeared. Bobby claimed to have received an anonymous call prior to the day with specific details.

The prosecutors stated that the suspect—Methuselah Savage—requested to meet on neutral territory to provide his account and to possibly clear his name to prevent potential arrest. Throughout the interview, Bobby made-up things as it went. He stated that the suspect Savage made up a multitude of incriminating remarks, enough to warrant an arrest then and there on the spot. He went further by saying it was at that point that he'd drawn his pistol on the suspect and ordered him to surrender without incident. The suspect grabbed a hold of a lamp and threw it at him, hitting him on the head, forcing him to shoot. Bobby also said that the suspect began to scramble for cover and tried to go for a weapon of his own he had situated under the mattress where the girl sat. This was how she'd suffered the gunshot wound inflicted upon her. Bobby planted a knife there for the cop to eventually find.

The head prosecutor of Dade County accepted all Bobby related without once questioning the truth or lack thereof of what he said. The two held the same position in the same profession. There became a deep degree of favoritism to go along with their acquaintance as well. They had to do everything possible from there to track down and arrest the fugitive suspect. New charges were put on Mickey. Bobby also had the Dade DA charge Peaches with, "Aiding and Abetting a Criminal," a felony count fixed upon her so as to have her remain in jail for a time being. Her bail was set very high to where she had no choice but to remain locked up until a trial was to begin, pregnant or not. Bobby did her duty. There was nothing she could do about it.

Fortunately for Peaches, the gunshot she suffered was onto the shoulder and not to the belly. She passed out from a panic attack. Medical personnel treated her at the hospital. They patched her up and released her to the police. The drama they were to go back and forth about seemed to only begin at that particular moment.

TO BE CONTINUED . . .

Lock Down Publications and Ca$h Presents
Assisted Publishing Packages

Due to an increase in the price of services we have increased our prices. The prices below reflect the price increase as of 11/1/24.

BASIC PACKAGE	UPGRADED PACKAGE
$699	**$1000**
Editing	Typing
Cover Design	Editing
Formatting	Cover Design
	Formatting
	Upload eBooks to Amazon
	Upload Paperback to Amazon
ADVANCE PACKAGE	**LDP SUPREME PACKAGE**
$1,400	**$1,700**
Typing	Typing
Editing (line editing/content)	Editing (line editing/content)
Cover Design	Cover Design
Formatting	Formatting
Copyright Registration	Copyright Registration
Proofreading	Proofreading
Upload eBooks to Amazon	Set up Amazon Account
Upload Paperback to Amazon	Upload eBooks to Amazon
	Upload Paperback to Amazon
	Advertise on LDP's Amazon and Facebook Page

***Other services available upon request.
Additional charges may apply

Lock Down Publications
P.O. Box 944
Stockbridge, GA 30281-9998
Phone: 470 303-9761
Email: lockdownpublications@gmail.com

Submission Guideline

Submit the first three chapters of your completed manuscript to ldpsubmissions@gmail.com. In the subject line add **Your Book's Title**. The manuscript must be in a Word Doc file and sent as an attachment. Document should be in Times New Roman, double spaced, and in size 12 font. Also, provide your synopsis and full contact information. If sending multiple submissions, they must each be in a separate email.

Have a story but no way to send it electronically? You can still submit to LDP/Ca$h Presents. Send in the first three chapters, written or typed, of your completed manuscript to:

LDP: Submissions Dept
P.O. Box 944
Stockbridge, GA 30281-9998

DO NOT send original manuscript. Must be a duplicate. Provide your synopsis and a cover letter containing your full contact information.

Thanks for considering LDP and Ca$h Presents.

NEW RELEASES

BLOODLINE OF A SAVAGE 1-3
THESE VICIOUS STREETS 1-3
RELENTLESS GOON 1-3
BY PRINCE A. TAUHID

THE BUTTERFLY MAFIA 1-3
BY FUMIYA PAYNE

A THUG'S STREET PRINCESS 1&2
BY MEESHA

CITY OF SMOKE 2
BY MOLOTTI

STEPPERS 1,2&3
THE REAL BADDIES OF CHI-RAQ
BY KING RIO

THE LANE 1&2
BY KEN-KEN SPENCE

THUG OF SPADES 1&2
LOVE IN THE TRENCHES 2
CORNER BOYS
BY COREY ROBINSON

TIL DEATH 3
BY ARYANNA

THE BIRTH OF A GANGSTER 4
BY DELMONT PLAYER

PRODUCT OF THE STREETS 1&2
BY DEMOND "MONEY" ANDERSON

NO TIME FOR ERROR
BY KEESE

MONEY HUNGRY DEMONS
BY TRANAY ADAMS

Coming Soon from Lock Down Publications/Ca$h Presents

IF YOU CROSS ME ONCE 6
ANGEL V
By Anthony Fields

IMMA DIE BOUT MINE 5
By Aryanna

A THUGS STREET PRINCESS 3
By Meesha

PRODUCT OF THE STREETS 3
By Demond Money Anderson

CORNER BOYS 2
By Corey Robinson

THE MURDER QUEENS 6&7
By Michael Gallon

CITY OF SMOKE 3
By Molotti

CONFESSIONS OF A DOPE BOY
By Nicholas Lock

THA TAKEOVER
By Keith Chandler

BETRAYAL OF A G 2
By Ray Vinci

CRIME BOSS
By Playa Ray

Available Now

RESTRAINING ORDER 1 & 2
By **CA$H & Coffee**

LOVE KNOWS NO BOUNDARIES 1-3
By **Coffee**

RAISED AS A GOON I, II, III & IV
BRED BY THE SLUMS I, II, III
BLAST FOR ME I & II
ROTTEN TO THE CORE I II III
A BRONX TALE I, II, III
DUFFLE BAG CARTEL I II III IV V VI
HEARTLESS GOON I II III IV V
A SAVAGE DOPEBOY I II
DRUG LORDS I II III
CUTTHROAT MAFIA I II
KING OF THE TRENCHES
By **Ghost**

LAY IT DOWN I & II
LAST OF A DYING BREED I II
BLOOD STAINS OF A SHOTTA I & II III
By **Jamaica**

LOYAL TO THE GAME I II III
LIFE OF SIN I, II III
By **TJ & Jelissa**

IF LOVING HIM IS WRONG…I & II

LOVE ME EVEN WHEN IT HURTS I II III
By **Jelissa**

PUSH IT TO THE LIMIT
By **Bre' Hayes**

BLOODY COMMAS I & II
SKI MASK CARTEL I, II & III
KING OF NEW YORK I II, III IV V
RISE TO POWER I II III
COKE KINGS I II III IV V
BORN HEARTLESS I II III IV
KING OF THE TRAP I II
By **T.J. Edwards**

WHEN THE STREETS CLAP BACK I & II III
THE HEART OF A SAVAGE I II III IV
MONEY MAFIA I II
LOYAL TO THE SOIL I II III
By **Jibril Williams**

A DISTINGUISHED THUG STOLE MY HEART I II & III
LOVE SHOULDN'T HURT I II III IV
RENEGADE BOYS 1-4
PAID IN KARMA 1-3
SAVAGE STORMS 1-3
AN UNFORESEEN LOVE 1-3
BABY, I'M WINTERTIME COLD 1-3
A THUG'S STREET PRINCESS 1&2
By **Meesha**

A GANGSTER'S CODE 1-3
A GANGSTER'S SYN 1-3
THE SAVAGE LIFE 1-3
CHAINED TO THE STREETS 1-3
BLOOD ON THE MONEY 1-3
A GANGSTA'S PAIN 1-3
BEAUTIFUL LIES AND UGLY TRUTHS

CHURCH IN THESE STREETS
By **J-Blunt**

CUM FOR ME 1-8
An LDP Erotica Collaboration

BLOOD OF A BOSS 1-5
SHADOWS OF THE GAME
TRAP BASTARD
By **Askari**

THE STREETS BLEED MURDER 1-3
THE HEART OF A GANGSTA 1-3
By **Jerry Jackson**

WHEN A GOOD GIRL GOES BAD
By **Adrienne**

THE COST OF LOYALTY 1-3
By **Kweli**

BRIDE OF A HUSTLA 1-3
THE FETTI GIRLS 1-3
CORRUPTED BY A GANGSTA 1-4
BLINDED BY HIS LOVE
THE PRICE YOU PAY FOR LOVE 1-3
DOPE GIRL MAGIC 1-3
By **Destiny Skai**

A KINGPIN'S AMBITION
A KINGPIN'S AMBITION II
I MURDER FOR THE DOUGH
By **Ambitious**

TRUE SAVAGE 1-7
DOPE BOY MAGIC 1-3
MIDNIGHT CARTEL 1-3
CITY OF KINGZ 1&2

NIGHTMARE ON SILENT AVE
THE PLUG OF LIL MEXICO 1&2
CLASSIC CITY
By **Chris Green**

A GANGSTER'S REVENGE 1-4
THE BOSS MAN'S DAUGHTERS 1-5
A SAVAGE LOVE 1&2
BAE BELONGS TO ME 1&2
A HUSTLER'S DECEIT 1-3
WHAT BAD BITCHES DO 1-3
SOUL OF A MONSTER 1-3
KILL ZONE
A DOPE BOY'S QUEEN 1-3
TIL DEATH 1-3
IMMA DIE BOUT MINE 1-4
By **Aryanna**

A DOPEBOY'S PRAYER
By **Eddie "Wolf" Lee**

THE KING CARTEL 1-3
By **Frank Gresham**

THESE NIGGAS AIN'T LOYAL 1-3
By **Nikki Tee**

GANGSTA SHYT 1-3
By **CATO**

THE ULTIMATE BETRAYAL
By **Phoenix**

BOSS'N UP 1-3
By **Royal Nicole**

I LOVE YOU TO DEATH

By **Destiny J**

I RIDE FOR MY HITTA
I STILL RIDE FOR MY HITTA
By **Misty Holt**

LOVE & CHASIN' PAPER
By **Qay Crockett**

TO DIE IN VAIN
SINS OF A HUSTLA
By **ASAD**

BROOKLYN HUSTLAZ
By **Boogsy Morina**

BROOKLYN ON LOCK 1 & 2
By **Sonovia**

GANGSTA CITY
By T**eddy Duke**

A DRUG KING AND HIS DIAMOND 1-3
A DOPEMAN'S RICHES
HER MAN, MINE'S TOO 1&2
CASH MONEY HO'S
THE WIFEY I USED TO BE 1&2
PRETTY GIRLS DO NASTY THINGS
By **Nicole Goosby**

LIPSTICK KILLAH 1-3
CRIME OF PASSION 1-3
FRIEND OR FOE 1-3
By **Mimi**

TRAPHOUSE KING 1-3
KINGPIN KILLAZ 1-3
STREET KINGS 1&2
PAID IN BLOOD 1&2

CARTEL KILLAZ 1-3
DOPE GODS 1&2
By **Hood Rich**

THE STREETS ARE CALLING
By **Duquie Wilson**

STEADY MOBBN' 1-3
THE STREETS STAINED MY SOUL 1-3
By **Marcellus Allen**

WHO SHOT YA 1-3
SON OF A DOPE FIEND 1-4
HEAVEN GOT A GHETTO 1&2
SKI MASK MONEY 1&2
By **Renta**

GORILLAZ IN THE BAY 1-4
TEARS OF A GANGSTA 1/&2
3X KRAZY 1&2
STRAIGHT BEAST MODE 1&2
By **DE'KARI**

TRIGGADALE 1-3
MURDA WAS THE CASE 1-3
By **Elijah R. Freeman**

SLAUGHTER GANG 1-3
RUTHLESS HEART 1-3
By **Willie Slaughter**

GOD BLESS THE TRAPPERS 1-3
THESE SCANDALOUS STREETS 1-3
FEAR MY GANGSTA 1-5
THESE STREETS DON'T LOVE NOBODY 1-2
BURY ME A G 1-5
A GANGSTA'S EMPIRE 1-4
THE DOPEMAN'S BODYGAURD 1&2
THE REALEST KILLAZ 1-3

THE LAST OF THE OGS 1-3
By **Tranay Adams**

MARRIED TO A BOSS 1-3
By **Destiny Skai & Chris Green**

KINGZ OF THE GAME 1-7
CRIME BOSS 1-3
By **Playa Ray**

FUK SHYT
By **Blakk Diamond**

DON'T F#CK WITH MY HEART 1&2
By **Linnea**

ADDICTED TO THE DRAMA 1-3
IN THE ARM OF HIS BOSS
By **Jamila**

LOYALTY AIN'T PROMISED 1&2
By **Keith Williams**

YAYO 1-4
A SHOOTER'S AMBITION 1&2
BRED IN THE GAME
By **S. Allen**

TRAP GOD 1-3
RICH $AVAGE 1-3
MONEY IN THE GRAVE 1-3
CARTEL MONEY
By **Martell Troublesome Bolden**

FOREVER GANGSTA 1&2
GLOCKS ON SATIN SHEETS 1&2
By **Adrian Dulan**

TOE TAGZ 1-4
LEVELS TO THIS SHYT 1&2
IT'S JUST ME AND YOU
By **Ah'Million**

KINGPIN DREAMS 1-3
RAN OFF ON DA PLUG
By **Paper Boi Rari**

THE STREETS MADE ME 1-3
By **Larry D. Wright**

CONFESSIONS OF A GANGSTA 1-4
CONFESSIONS OF A JACKBOY 1-3
CONFESSIONS OF A HITMAN
By **Nicholas Lock**

I'M NOTHING WITHOUT HIS LOVE
SINS OF A THUG
TO THE THUG I LOVED BEFORE
A GANGSTA SAVED XMAS
IN A HUSTLER I TRUST
By **Monet Dragun**

QUIET MONEY 1-3
THUG LIFE 1-3
EXTENDED CLIP 1&2
A GANGSTA'S PARADISE
By **Trai'Quan**

CAUGHT UP IN THE LIFE 1-3
THE STREETS NEVER LET GO 1-3
By **Robert Baptiste**

NEW TO THE GAME 1-3
MONEY, MURDER & MEMORIES 1-3
By **Malik D. Rice**

CREAM 2-3
THE STREETS WILL TALK
By **Yolanda Moore**

THE STREETS WILL NEVER CLOSE 1-3
By **K'ajji**

LIFE OF A SAVAGE 1-4
A GANGSTA'S QUR'AN 1-4
MURDA SEASON 1-3
GANGLAND CARTEL 1-3
CHI'RAQ GANGSTAS 1-4
KILLERS ON ELM STREET 1-3
JACK BOYZ N DA BRONX 1-3
A DOPEBOY'S DREAM 1-3
JACK BOYS VS DOPE BOYS 1-3
COKE GIRLZ
COKE BOYS
SOSA GANG 1&2
BRONX SAVAGES
BODYMORE KINGPINS
BLOOD OF A GOON
By **Romell Tukes**

CONCRETE KILLA 1-3
VICIOUS LOYALTY 1-3
By **Kingpen**

THE ULTIMATE SACRIFICE 1-6
KHADIFI
IF YOU CROSS ME ONCE 1-3
ANGEL 1-4
IN THE BLINK OF AN EYE
By **Anthony Fields**

THE LIFE OF A HOOD STAR
By **Ca$h & Rashia Wilson**

NIGHTMARES OF A HUSTLA 1-3

BLOOD AND GAMES 1&2
By **King Dream**

GHOST MOB
By **Stilloan Robinson**

HARD AND RUTHLESS 1&2
MOB TOWN 251
THE BILLIONAIRE BENTLEYS 1-3
REAL G'S MOVE IN SILENCE
By **Von Diesel**

MOB TIES 1-7
SOUL OF A HUSTLER, HEART OF A KILLER 1-3
GORILLAZ IN THE TRENCHES
By **SayNoMore**

BODYMORE MURDERLAND 1-3
THE BIRTH OF A GANGSTER 1-4
By **Delmont Player**

FOR THE LOVE OF A BOSS 1&2
By **C. D. Blue**

KILLA KOUNTY 1-5
By **Khufu**

MOBBED UP 1-4
THE BRICK MAN 1-5
THE COCAINE PRINCESS 1-10
STEPPERS 1-3
SUPER GREMLIN 1-4
By **King Rio**

MONEY GAME 1&2
By **Smoove Dolla**

A GANGSTA'S KARMA 1-4

SAVAGE FAMILY EMPIRE | PRINCE A. TAUHID

By **FLAME**

KING OF THE TRENCHES 1-3
By **GHOST & TRANAY ADAMS**

QUEEN OF THE ZOO 1&2
By **Black Migo**

GRIMEY WAYS 1-3
BETRAYAL OF A G
By **Ray Vinci**

XMAS WITH AN ATL SHOOTER
By **Ca$h & Destiny Skai**

KING KILLA 1&2
By **Vincent "Vitto" Holloway**

BETRAYAL OF A THUG 1&2
By **Fre$h**

THE MURDER QUEENS 1-5
By **Michael Gallon**

FOR THE LOVE OF BLOOD 1-4
By **Jamel Mitchell**

HOOD CONSIGLIERE 1&2
NO TIME FOR ERROR
By **Keese**

PROTÉGÉ OF A LEGEND 1&2
LOVE IN THE TRENCHES 1&2
By **Corey Robinson**

THE PLUG'S RUTHLESS DAUGHTER
By **Tony Daniels**

SAVAGE FAMILY EMPIRE | PRINCE A. TAUHID

BORN IN THE GRAVE 1-3
CRIME PAYS
By **Self Made Tay**

MOAN IN MY MOUTH
By **XTASY**

TORN BETWEEN A GANGSTER AND A GENTLEMAN
By **J-BLUNT & Miss Kim**

LOYALTY IS EVERYTHING 1-3
CITY OF SMOKE 1&2
By **Molotti**

HERE TODAY GONE TOMORROW 1&2
By **Fly Rock**

WOMEN LIE MEN LIE 1-4
FIFTY SHADES OF SNOW 1-3
STACK BEFORE YOU SPLURGE
GIRLS FALL LIKE DOMINOES
NAÏVE TO THE STREETS
By **ROY MILLIGAN**

PILLOW PRINCESS
By **S. Hawkins**

THE BUTTERFLY MAFIA 1-3
SALUTE MY SAVAGERY 1&2
By **Fumiya Payne**

THE LANE 1&2
By **Ken-Ken Spence**

THE PUSSY TRAP 1-5
By **Nene Capri**

DIRTY DNA
By **Blaque**

SANCTIFIED AND HORNY
by **XTASY**

BOOKS BY LDP'S CEO, CA$H

TRUST IN NO MAN
TRUST IN NO MAN 2
TRUST IN NO MAN 3
BONDED BY BLOOD
SHORTY GOT A THUG
THUGS CRY
THUGS CRY 2
THUGS CRY 3
TRUST NO BITCH
TRUST NO BITCH 2
TRUST NO BITCH 3
TIL MY CASKET DROPS
RESTRAINING ORDER
RESTRAINING ORDER 2
IN LOVE WITH A CONVICT
LIFE OF A HOOD STAR
XMAS WITH AN ATL SHOOTER